"Are you all

didn't mean to

"I'm not angry; I'm hot." Water sloshed in the jug. Beulah eyed the sweaty man. "You look hotter." Without pausing for reflection, she dashed the water into his face.

Water dripped from his nose and beard and trickled down his chest. "Did I deserve that?"

He didn't seem angry. A nervous giggle escaped before Beulah could stop it. "You needed a bath."

His eyes flared, and Beulah knew she had better get moving. Picking up her skirts, she dashed for the fence, intending to vanish into the forest. But an arm caught her around the waist. "Not so fast." Without further ceremony he tossed her over his shoulder and picked up the empty jar. Her book flew into the tall grass.

"What are you doing?" she gasped. "Put me down!" He surmounted the fence without apparent difficulty and headed into the woods.

Beulah found it hard to breathe while hanging head down over his shoulder, and her stomach muscles were too weak to lift her upper body for long. In order to draw a good breath she had to put both hands on his back and push herself up. "Myles, a gentleman doesn't treat a lady this way! Please put me down. This is. . .improper!"

JILL STENGL recently moved to Wisconsin where her family built a log home, glad to have years of moving with the military behind them. Jill considers herself a homebody and enjoys home schooling the three youngest of her four children, sewing, drawing, and taking long walks with her husband and Fritz, a miniature schnauzer. She writes inspirational romance because that's what she most enjoys reading, and she believes that everything she does should be glorifying to God.

HEARTSONG PRESENTS

Books by Jill Stengl
HP197—Eagle Pilot
HP222—Finally, Love
HP292—A Child of Promise
HP335—Time for a Miracle
HP387—Grant Me Mercy

Myles from Anywhere

Jill Stengl

Heartsong Presents

With love to Tom, Annie, Jimmy, and Peter Stengl. I thank God for each of you every day. Every mother should be so blessed!

Thank you again to Paula Pruden Macha and Pamela Griffin—two living proofs that long-distance friendship is possible. Love you both!

A note from the author:

I love to hear from my readers! You may correspond with me by writing:

Jill Stengl
Author Relations
PO Box 719
Uhrichsville, OH 44683

ISBN 1-58660-205-5

MYLES FROM ANYWHERE

All Scripture quotations, unless otherwise noted, are taken from the King James Version of the Bible.

Cover illustration by Gary Maria.

PRINTED IN THE U.S.A.

prologue

1872

CHILD PRODIGY MISSING. STATEWIDE SEARCH UNDERWAY FOR MYLES VAN HUYSEN, MUSICAL STAR, read the headlines of the August 21 edition of the city paper. A passerby stepped on the newspaper where it lay crumpled beside the tent door, and a breeze lifted the top page, sending it drifting across the midway.

A boy glared at the paper from beneath the brim of his cap, hoping his prospective employer had not read it closely. Why did Gram have to make such a big deal about everything?

"You say you're willing to work hard, Kid? How old are you, anyway?"

"Eighteen. Ain't got no family." He struggled to sound illiterate yet mature enough to merit the two extra years he claimed.

"Kinda puny, ain't ya?" The owner of the traveling circus chomped on his unlit cigar. "You're in luck, Red. One of our fellas went down sick a week back, and we've been struggling since. It ain't easy work, and the pay is peanuts, but you'll get room and board, such as it is. Go see Parker in the animal tent and tell him I sent you."

"Yes, Mr. Bonacelli. Thank you, Mr. Bonacelli."

"You may not be thankin' me when you find out what you'll be doin'. What's yer name, Red?"

"Myles Trent." It was his name minus its third element. If he so much as mentioned "Van Huysen" the game would end for certain.

"Hmph. I'll call ya Red."

Visions of becoming an acrobat or animal trainer soon vanished from Myles's head. During the next few months, he worked harder than he had ever worked in his life, cleaning animal pens. It was nasty and hazardous work at times, yet he enjoyed becoming friends with other circus employees. Whenever the circus picked up to move to the next town, everyone worked together, from the clowns to the trapeze artists to the bearded lady. It wasn't long before Myles began to move up in the circus world.

Bonacelli's Circus made its way south from New York, then west toward Ohio, playing in towns along the highways and railroads. During the coldest months, the caravans headed south along the Mississippi; spring found them headed north. Months passed into a year.

Lengthening his face to minimize creases, Myles wiped grease paint from his eyelids. Behind him, the tent flap was pulled aside. Someone came in. "Antonio?" he guessed.

"Hello, Myles."

His eyes popped open. A handsome face smiled at him from his mirror.

Myles froze. His shoulders drooped. He turned on the stool. "Monte."

The brothers stared at each other. Monte pulled up a chair and straddled it backward. "I caught today's show. Never thought I'd see my musician brother doing flips onto a horse's back. You've built muscle and calluses. Look healthier than I can remember." There was grudging admiration in his voice.

"The acrobats and clowns taught me tricks."

"I've been hanging around, asking questions. People like and respect you. Say you're honest and hardworking."

Myles's eyes narrowed. "I love the circus, Monte. I like making people happy."

"You're a performer. It's in your blood."

Myles turned to his mirror and rubbed blindly at the paint. "Why so pleasant all of a sudden?"

Monte ignored the question. "Gram wants you back. She's already spent too much on detectives. I'll write and tell her I found you before she fritters away our fortune."

"I'm not going back."

"I didn't ask you to. The old lady sent me to keep an eye on you. She never said I had to go back. . .at least not right away." One of Monte's brows lifted, and he gave Myles his most charming smile. "The Van Huysen Soap Company and fortune will wait for me. No reason to waste my youth in a stuffy office, learning business from a fat family friend. I think I'd rather be a circus star like my runny-nosed kid brother."

"You've seen me. Now get lost." Hope faded from Myles's eyes. "You'll spoil everything."

"Believe it or not, I do understand. That was no life for a kid. I've often wondered how you endured it as long as you did. Getting out of that Long Island goldfish bowl is a relief. Always someone watching, moralizing, planning your life—whew! You had the right idea. I could hardly believe my luck when Gram sent me after you."

"She trusted you," Myles observed dryly. "What are you planning to do?"

"Does this circus need more workers? I'm serious. This looks like the life for me."

Myles huffed. "Nobody needs a worker like you, Monte. Why don't you go find yourself a gaming hall and forget you ever had a brother?"

"Gram would never forgive me if I returned without you."

"You could tell her I'm dead."

Monte pondered the idea in mock gravity, dark eyes twinkling. "Tempting, but impossible. Family honor and all that. You'd show up someday, then I'd look the dolt at best, the knave at worst. Part of the family fortune is yours, you know. I wouldn't try to filch it from you. I'm not as rotten as you think, little brother. I do feel some responsibility for my nitwit prodigy sibling."

The next morning when Monte left his borrowed bunk, Myles was gone. No one had seen him leave. Running a big hand down his face, Monte swore. "Gotta find that crazy kid!"

❦

"Are you here with good news or bad, George Poole?" the old lady grumbled from her seat in a faded armchair. A few coals glowed upon the hearth near her feet. "I trust you have disturbed my afternoon rest for good reason."

"Yes, Mrs. Van Huysen. You may see for yourself." He thrust a newspaper into her hands and pointed at a paragraph near the bottom of the page. "An associate of mine in Milwaukee—that's a town in Wisconsin—heard of my quest, spotted this article, and mailed the paper to me."

"Kind of him," Mrs. Van Huysen said, fumbling to put on her glasses. Holding the folded-back paper near her face, she blinked. "For what am I looking?"

"This, Madam. The article concerns a small-town farmer who, years ago, served a prison sentence for robbery and murder. Last summer, new evidence was discovered and the man's name was cleared of the crimes. Judging by the article's tone, this Obadiah Watson appears to be a fine Christian man. It is a pleasure when justice is served, is it not?"

"Yes, yes, but what has this to do with my grandsons?" Virginia Van Huysen struggled to keep her patience.

"Let me find the line. . .ah, right here. You see? The article mentions a certain Myles Trent, hired laborer on Watson's farm." Poole's eyes scanned his client's face.

"I fail to see the significance, Mr. Poole. You raised my hopes for this?"

"Don't you see, Madam? Your grandson's name is Myles Trent Van Huysen. Oftentimes a man in hiding will use a pseudonym, and what could be easier to recall than one's own given name?"

"Have you any proof that this man is my Myles? And what of Monte? There is no word of him in this article. The last I heard from the boys, they were together in Texas. Isn't Wisconsin way up north somewhere? Why ever would Myles be there?" Pulling a lacy handkerchief from her cuff, Virginia dabbed at her eyes. "In Monte's last letter he told me that he had surrendered his life to the Lord. Why, then, did he stop writing to me? I don't understand it."

Poole tugged his muttonchop whiskers. "I cannot say, dear madam. The particular region of Texas described in your grandson's most recent letters is a veritable wasteland. Our efforts there were vain; my people discovered no information about your grandsons. It was as if they had dropped from the face of the earth."

"Except for the note your partner sent me about the game hunter in Wyoming." Virginia's tone was inquisitive.

"An unfortunate mistake on Mr. Wynter's part. He should have waited until he had obtained more solid information before consulting you. Be that as it may, Madam, unless this Myles Trent proves to be your relation, I fear I must persuade you to give up this quest. I dislike taking your money for naught."

"Naught?" Virginia lifted her pince-nez to give him a quelling look.

Poole nodded. "We at Poole, Poole, and Wynter are ever reluctant to admit defeat, yet I fear we may be brought to that unfortunate pass. It has been nine years since Myles disappeared and nearly six since Monte's last letter reached you. If your grandsons are yet living, they are twenty-five and twenty-eight now."

"I can do simple addition, Mr. Poole," Virginia said. "Have you given up entirely on that hunter?"

"The fellow disappeared. He was probably an outlaw who became nervous when Wynter started asking questions. You must keep in mind that your grandsons are no longer children to be brought home and disciplined. They are men and entitled to live the lives they choose. I fear Myles's concert career will never resume."

Virginia clenched her jaw and lifted a defiant chin. "I would spend my last cent to find my boys. Look into this, Mr. Poole, and may the Lord be with you."

one

Shall not God search this out?
For he knoweth the secrets of the heart.
Psalm 44:21

Summer 1881

"Move over, Marigold."

The Jersey cow munched on her breakfast, eyes half closed. When Myles pushed on her side, she shifted in the stall, giving him room for his milking stool and bucket. Settling on the stool, he rested his forehead on Marigold's flank, grasped her teats, and gently kneaded her udder while squeezing. His hands were already warm since she was the sixth cow he had milked that morning. Marigold let down her milk, and the warm liquid streamed into the bucket. Myles had learned that it paid to be patient with the cows; they rewarded his kindness with their cooperation.

"Meow!" A furry body twined around his ankle, rumbling a purr that reminded Myles of a passing freight train. Other cats peered at Myles from all sides—from the hayloft, around the stall walls, from the top of Marigold's stanchion. Their eyes seldom blinked.

The plump gray and white cat had perfected her technique. She bumped her face against Myles's knee, reached a velvet paw to touch his elbow, and blinked sweetly.

"Nice try, you pushy cat, but you've got to wait your turn. I'll give a saucer to all of you when I'm finished."

"Why do you reward them for begging? It only makes them worse." A deep voice spoke from the next stall where Al Moore was milking another cow.

"Guess I like cats."

"I. . .um, Myles, I've got to tell you that I'll be heading over to Cousin Buck's farm after dinner. I've got to talk with Beulah today. . .you know, about my letter."

"I'll be there too. I'm working in Buck's barn this afternoon—mending harnesses and such."

"Things have changed since Cousin Buck married Violet Fairfield last year and took over her farm, Fairfield's Folly," Al commented sadly. "I mean, in the old days he kept up with every detail about our farm, but he's too busy being a husband and papa these days."

"He doesn't miss much. Must be hard work, running the two farms." Myles defended his friend.

"I run this place myself," Al protested. After a moment's silence he added, "You're right; I shouldn't complain. I just miss the old days; that's all. Anyway, to give Cousin Buck credit, being Beulah's stepfather must be a job in itself, and now with Buck and Violet's new baby. . ." His voice trailed away. "Buck has made major improvements at the Folly farm this past year. Guess that's no surprise to you."

"I do have firsthand knowledge of those improvements," Myles acknowledged. "Working at both farms keeps me hopping, but I don't mind. I'm glad Buck is happily married. I've never worked for better people than you and your cousin."

"Since I'm taking the afternoon off, I'll handle the milking this evening. How's that?" Al asked. "Don't want you to think I'm shirking."

Myles smiled to himself. "Don't feel obligated, Boss. You always do your share of the work. Be good for you to take a few hours to play."

"But you never do. Wish you'd relax some; then I wouldn't feel guilty."

"Maybe you and I could toss a baseball around with Samuel this afternoon." The prospect lifted Myles's spirits. He liked nothing better than to spend time with Obadiah "Buck" Watson's three stepchildren. The retired cowboy preferred to be called "Obie," but Myles had known him for years as "Buck" and found it impossible to address or even think of his boss by any other name.

"That would be great!" Al sounded like an overgrown schoolboy.

Myles stripped the last drops from Marigold's teats. Rising, he patted the cow's bony rump. "You're a good girl, Goldie." He nearly tripped over the pushy gray cat as he left the stall. With a trill of expectation, it trotted ahead of him toward the milk cans, where several other felines had already congregated.

Myles found the chipped saucer beneath a bench. Sliding it to the open floor with one foot, he tipped the bucket and poured a stream of milk—on top of a gray and white head. Myles smiled as the cat retreated under the bench, shaking her head and licking as much of her white ruff as she could reach. Another cat began to assist her, removing the milk from the back of her head. "Pushy cat, Pushy cat, where have you been?" Myles crooned.

He filled the saucer until it overflowed; yet it was polished clean within seconds. A few cats had to content themselves with licking drops from the floor or from their companions. Myles tried to count the swarming animals but lost track at twelve.

"Too many cats," Al remarked, emptying his bucket into a can.

"They keep down the rodent population," Myles said.

"I know, but the barn's getting overcrowded. There were a lot of kittens born in the spring, but most of them are gone. I don't know if they just died or if something killed them."

Myles squatted and Pushy cat hopped into his lap, kneading his thigh with her paws and blinking her yellow eyes. She seemed to enjoy rubbing her face against his beard. He stroked her smooth back and enjoyed that rumbling purr. Myles knew Al was right, but neither man had an answer for the problem.

"Say, Myles, what if. . .I mean, are you. . .do you have any plans to move on? Might you be willing to stay on here over the winter and. . .I'm not sure how to say this." Al ran long fingers through his hair, staring at the barn floor.

Myles rubbed the cat and waited for Al to find the words. He had a fair idea what was coming.

"I'm hoping to marry Beulah and take her to California with me—to meet my parents, you know. We would probably be gone for close to a year, and I can't leave Cousin Buck to run both this place and Fairfield's Folly alone. I would take it kindly if you would. . .well, run my farm as if it were yours, just while I'm away, you understand. I would make it worth your while. You don't need to answer me now; take your time to think it over."

Myles nodded. In spite of his determination to keep his own counsel, one question escaped. "Have you asked her yet?"

"Asked Beulah? Not yet." Al's boots shifted on the floorboards. "That's the other thing that worries me. She's. . .uh. . . I don't know that she'll take to the idea of a quick wedding. We've never discussed marriage. . .but she must know I plan to marry her. Everyone knows."

Myles glanced at his young boss's face. "Will you go if she refuses?"

Al looked uncertain. "I could marry her when I get back, but I hate to leave things hanging. Another man could come along and steal her away from me. Maybe I could ask her to wait." He collapsed on the bench, propped his elbows on his spread knees, and rested his chin on one fist. "She's really not a flirt, but I can't seem to pin her down. Every time I try to be serious, she changes the subject. What should I do, Myles?"

Myles rose to his feet and began to rub his flat stomach with one hand. "You're asking an old bachelor for courtship advice?" He hoped the irony in his voice escaped Al's notice. "I've got no experience with women."

"No experience at all?" Al's face colored. "I mean. . .uh. . . Sorry."

Myles shrugged. "No offense taken. I left home at sixteen

and bummed around the country for years."

"What did you do to keep alive?"

"Any work I could find. No time or opportunity to meet a decent woman and had enough sense to avoid the other kind. When I drifted farther west it was the same. You don't see a lot of women wandering the wilderness."

"So where are you from?"

"Anywhere and everywhere." His lips twitched into a smile that didn't reach his eyes. "When your cousin hired me and brought me here to Longtree, that was the first time I'd been around women since I was a kid. Guess I don't know how to behave around females."

"I didn't know you were afraid of women. Is that why you almost never go to church or socials?"

Myles lifted a brow. "I didn't say I was afraid of them. More like they're afraid of me."

"If you'd smile and use sentences of more than one syllable, they might discover you're a decent fellow."

This prompted a genuine smile. "I'll try it. Any other advice?"

Al cocked his head and grinned. "That depends on which female has caught your eye. Want to confide in old Al?"

"I'd better cast about first and see if any female will have me," Myles evaded.

Al chuckled. "Too late. I know about you and Marva Obermeier."

"About me and. . .whom?"

"Don't look so surprised. Since the barn raising at Obermeiers' when you and she talked for an hour, everyone in town knows. She's a nice lady. If you want a little extra to hold and like a woman who'll do all the talking, Marva is for you."

"But that was—" Myles began to protest.

"Things aren't progressing the way you want, eh? You ought to spend evenings getting to know her family, getting comfortable in the home. Try teasing her and see what happens. Nice teasing, I mean. Women enjoy that kind of attention from a man."

"They do?"

A collie burst through the open barn door. Panicked cats scattered. Both men chuckled. "Good work, Treat."

Treat grinned and wagged half her body along with her tail, eager to herd the cows to pasture. "Cats are beneath your notice, eh, Girl?" Al said, ruffling her ears.

Al carried the milk cans to the dairy. Myles untied the cows and directed Treat to gather them and start them ambling along the path.

Udders swaying, bells clanging, gray noses glistening, the cows did their best to ignore the furry pest at their heels. While Myles held the pasture gate open, Treat encouraged the little herd to pass through. Myles gave one bony bovine a swat before latching the gate behind her. "As usual, last in line. No wandering off today, my ornery old girl."

The sun was still low in the sky and already the temperature was rising. Myles swung his arms in circles to relieve the kinks. He glanced around. No one watching. He performed a few cartwheels, a round off, then a front flip to back flip in one quick motion. He straightened in triumph, flushed and pleased, arms lifted to greet the morning. The cows and Treat were unimpressed.

"Good thing you're used to my antics. Hey, Treat, maybe I'll see Beulah today." Myles slapped his thighs until the dog placed her front paws on them. He ruffled her fur with both hands. "What do you think, Girl? Think Beulah will smile at me?"

Then his grin faded and his heavy boots scuffed in the dirt. Little chance of that while Al was around. Of all the stupid things Myles had ever done, falling in love with his boss's girl was undoubtedly the worst.

❦

Deep in thought, Beulah Fairfield dumped used dishwater behind her mother's gladiolus. Something jabbed into her ribs, and the last of the water flew skyward. "Oh!" She spun around, slapping away reaching hands. "Al, stop it!"

Al took the two back steps in a single bound and held the

kitchen door for her. "Testy woman. Better make myself useful and return to her good graces."

She was tempted to suggest that he choose another time to visit, but her mother had chided her several times recently for rudeness. "Thanks." Beulah forced a smile as she entered the kitchen before him. His return smile seemed equally fake. "Is something wrong, Al?"

He let the door slam behind him. "Nothing much."

Beulah hung the dishpan on its hook and arranged the dishtowels on the back of the stove to dry. "Would you like a cup of coffee?"

"Uh, sure. Yes, please."

"Please take a seat at the table, and I will join you presently."

In another minute, she set down his coffee and seated herself across the table from him. His forehead was pale where his hat usually hid it from the sun; his dark hair looked freshly combed. Beulah knew her apron was spotted, but she was too self-conscious to change to a fresh one in front of Al. Her hair must be a sight—straggling about her face. "I've been canning tomatoes all morning." She indicated the glowing red jars lining the sideboard.

Before Al could comment, Beulah's sister Eunice burst into the room. The hall door hit the wall and china rattled on the oak dresser. "It *was* your voice I heard in here! Why did you sneak around to the back door, Al? I was watching for you out front."

A black and white dog slipped in behind Eunice and thrust her nose into Al's hand, brushy tail beating against the table legs. "Watchful, shame on you! Get out of the kitchen." Beulah attempted to shoo the dog away.

"She's all right." Petting the dog, Al gave Eunice a halfhearted smile. "I didn't sneak. My horse is in the barn, big as life. I rode over with Myles. He's mending the whiffletree the horse kicked apart while we were pulling stumps."

"Myles is in our barn?" Beulah asked.

"Still want to go for a ride today, do you?" Al asked Eunice as if Beulah had not spoken.

The girl flopped down in the chair beside him. "Of course we want to ride with you. My brother has to finish cleaning the chicken pen, but he's almost done. I finished my chores. Won't you teach me to jump today? Please?" She laid her head on Al's shoulder and gave him her best pleading gaze, batting long lashes.

He chuckled and roughed up her brown curls. "Subtle, aren't you, Youngster? We'll see. I'd better talk to your parents before we try jumping. To be honest, Blue Eyes, I want to talk with your sister in private for a minute, so could—"

The door popped open again, this time admitting Violet Fairfield Watson, the girls' mother, with a wide-eyed baby propped upon her shoulder. "Would one of you please take Daniel while I change his bedclothes?" She transferred the baby to Beulah's reaching arms. "Thank you, Dear. Hello, Albert. Will you stay for supper tonight?"

"I. . .um, thank you, but no, not tonight, Ma'am. I. . .I've got to do the milking. I promised the kids we'd go for a ride this afternoon, but then I've got to get home and. . .and get some work done."

Violet gave him a searching look. "Hmm. Is something wrong, Al?"

Blood colored his face right up to his hairline. "Actually, yes. I got a letter from my mother yesterday. She wants me to come home to California. I'm the oldest son, you know. It's been five years since I was last home, and my folks want to see me again."

"I see." Violet Watson sent Beulah a quick glance before asking Al: "Do you plan to leave soon?"

"I'm not sure, Ma'am. That depends. . .on a lot of things. I'll have to work out a plan with Cousin Buck—Obie—for care of the farm. I can't expect Myles to handle everything alone for so long. I mean, he's just a hired hand."

"How long is 'so long'?" Eunice asked, her expression frozen.

"I don't know. Could be up to a year. The train fare

between here and California is no laughing matter. I have to make the visit worth the price."

"Yes, you do need to speak with Obie about this, Al." Violet looked concerned. "That is a long time to leave your farm."

Al held out his hands, fingers spread. "I know, but what else can I do? They're my parents."

"But, Al, a whole year? What will we do without you?" Eunice wailed.

Wrapping one long arm around the girl, Al pressed her head to his shoulder. "Miss me, I hope. I'll be back, Blue Eyes. Never fear."

Rocking her baby brother in her arms, Beulah watched Al embrace her sister. *No more pokes in the ribs, no more mawkish stares. I wonder how soon he will leave?*

Baby Daniel began to fuss. Beulah took the excuse to leave the kitchen and wandered through the house, bouncing him on her hip. He waved his arms and kicked her in the thighs, chortling. She heard the others still talking, their voices muffled by intervening doors.

My friends all think I'm the luckiest girl in the world because Al likes me. He is handsome, nice, loves God, has his own farm—he'll make a great husband for someone. But that someone isn't me!

She strolled back into the hall, studying the closed kitchen door. No one would notice if she slipped outside. Snatching a basket from a hook on the hall tree, she headed for the barn. Her heart thumped far more rapidly than this mild exertion required. Shifting Daniel higher on her hip, she reached for her hair and winced. No bonnet, and hair like an osprey's nest. Oh, well; too late now. If she didn't hurry, Myles might finish his work and leave before she had a chance to see him.

A tingle skittered down her spine. Without turning her head, she knew that Myles stood in the barn doorway. The man's gaze was like a fist squeezing her lungs until she gasped for air. Daniel squawked and thumped his hand against Beulah's chest. He managed to grasp one of her buttons and tried to pull it to his mouth, diving toward it. Beulah had just enough presence of mind to catch him before he plunged out of her arms.

One ankle turned as she approached the barn, and she staggered. Daniel transferred his attention to the basket hanging from her arm beneath him. He reached for it and once more nearly escaped Beulah's grasp. "Daniel, stop that," she snapped in exasperation, feeling bedraggled and clumsy.

"Need a hand?"

Swallowing hard, Beulah lifted her gaze. A little smile curled Myles's lips. One hand rubbed the bib of his overalls. The shadow of his hat hid his eyes, yet she felt them burning into her.

"I came for eggs," she said, brushing hair from her face, then hoisting Daniel higher on her hip. "For custard."

"Your brother Sam headed for the house with a basket of eggs not two minutes back."

"He did?" Beulah felt heat rush into her face. "I didn't see him."

Daniel grabbed at a button again, then mouthed Beulah's cheek and chin. She felt his wet lips and heard the fond little "Ahh" he always made when he gave her kisses. Unable to ignore the baby's overtures, she kissed his soft cheek. "I love you, too, Daniel. Now hold still."

When she looked up, white teeth gleamed through Myles's sun-bleached beard. "Thought Al was with you."

"He's in the kitchen with my mother and Eunice. Daniel and I came out for the eggs. Are you—will you be here long?"

"Might play baseball with Samuel and Al. Glad you came out for a visit."

Myles appeared to choose his words with care, and his voice. . .that rich voice curled her toes. Did he know she had come outside in hope of seeing him? Why must her mind palpitate along with her body whenever Myles was near? She was incapable either of analyzing his comments or of giving a lucid reply.

"You haven't been to our house for awhile, and I haven't

seen you at church all summer."

His smile faded. He took a step closer, then stopped. Did Myles feel the pull, almost like a noose tightening around the two of them and drawing them ever closer together? She had never been this close to him before. Only five or six feet of dusty earth separated them.

Tired of being ignored, Daniel let out a screech and smacked Beulah's mouth with a slimy hand. Pain and anger flashed; she struggled to hide both. "Daniel, don't hit."

The baby's face crumpled, and he began to wail. Sucking in her lip, Beulah tasted blood. "I think it's time for his nap." She spoke above Daniel's howls. "I'll try to come back later."

Myles nodded, waved one hand, and vanished into the barn's shadows. Beulah trotted toward the house, patting Daniel's back. "Hush, Sweetie. Beulah isn't angry with you. I know you're tired and hungry. We'll find Mama, and everything will be fine."

Al held the door open for her. "What are you doing out here? What's wrong with the little guy?"

"Where's my mother?"

"Upstairs. You going riding with us?" he called.

"No, you go on. I've got work to do." She barely paused on the bottom step.

"Play ball with us later?"

"Maybe." Beulah hid her grin in Daniel's soft hair.

Once Daniel was content in his mother's arms, Beulah returned to the kitchen to work and ponder. Sure enough, a basket of brown eggs waited on the floor beside the butter churn. Samuel must have entered the kitchen right after she left it.

Beulah found her mother's custard recipe on a stained card and began to collect the ingredients. *I'm just imagining that Myles admires me. Probably he watches everyone that way. I scarcely know the man. No one knows much about him. He could be from anywhere—a bank robber or desperado for all we know. It is ridiculous to moon about him when I can have a man like Al with a snap of my fingers. Myles is beneath me socially—probably never went to school. Could never support a family—we would live in a shack. . .*

Al's words repeated in her mind: *Just a hired hand. Just a hired hand. Just a hired hand. . .*

two

And when ye stand praying, forgive,
if ye have ought against any:
that your Father also which is in heaven
may forgive you your trespasses.
Mark 11:25

Custard cooled on the windowsill. Untying her apron, Beulah peeked through the kitchen window. Outside, a baseball smacked into a leather glove. She heard her brother Samuel's shrill voice and good-natured joking between Al and Myles. *He's still here!* She hung her apron on a hook, smoothed her skirts, and straightened her shoulders. Once again, her heart began to pound.

Eunice slammed open the kitchen door. Damp curls plastered her forehead; scarlet cheeks intensified the blue of her eyes. "We had a great ride, Beulah! You should have come."

Beulah wrinkled her nose.

Eunice splashed her face at the pump. "It hurts Al's feelings that you never want to ride with us."

"I'm sure I don't know why."

Lifting her face from the towel, Eunice protested, "But you're supposed to want to spend time with him. People in love want to be together all the time, don't they?"

"How would I know?" Beulah said. "And I can't see how being in love would make me want to ride a horse. Hmph. You need a bath. I can smell horse from here."

"You're mean, Beulah." Eunice rushed from the room.

Beulah rolled her eyes. Pinching her cheeks, she checked her reflection in the tiny mirror over the washbasin. "Guess I didn't need to pinch my cheeks. They're already hot as fire."

Beyond Beulah's kitchen garden, the two men and Samuel formed a triangle around the yard. The ball smacked into Al's glove. He tossed it to Samuel, easing his throw for the boy's sake. Samuel hurled it at Myles, who fielded it at his ankles, then fired another bullet toward Al. Around and around they went, never tiring of the game.

"Hi, Beulah!" Al greeted her with a wave. "Want to play? We've got an extra mitt."

"No, thank you." *He must be crazy.* "Don't want to spoil your fun."

"We would throw easy to you," Samuel assured her.

"I'll watch." Beulah moved to the swing her stepfather Obie had hung from a tall elm. After tucking up her skirt lest it drag in the dust, she began to swing. The men seemed unaware of her scrutiny. They bantered with Samuel and harassed each other. Her gaze shifted from Myles to Al and back again.

Al's long, lean frame had not yet filled out with muscle. A thatch of black hair, smooth brown skin, beautiful dark eyes, and a flashing smile made him an object of female fascination. How many times had Beulah been told of her incredible good luck in snaring his affection? She had lost count.

Leaning back in the swing, she pumped harder, hearing her skirts flap in the wind. Overhead, blue sky framed oak, maple, and elm leaves. A woodpecker tapped out his message on a dead birch.

Sitting straight, she wrapped her arms around the ropes and fixed her gaze upon Myles. He was grinning. Beulah felt her heart skip a beat. Myles had the cutest, funniest laugh—a rare treat to hear. What would he look like without that bushy beard? He had a trim build—not as short and slim as her stepfather Obie, but nowhere near as tall as Al.

The ongoing conversation penetrated her thoughts. "So are you planning to go, Al? Will you take me with you? I've always wanted to see a circus. I bet my folks would let me go with you," Samuel cajoled.

Al glanced toward Beulah. "I was thinking I might go. It's playing in Bolger all weekend. The parade arrives tomorrow."

Samuel let out a whoop. "Let's all go together! Eunice wants to go, and you do, don't you, Beulah? Will you come, too, Myles? Maybe they'll ask you to be a clown. Myles can do lots of tricks, you know. Show 'em how you walk on your hands. Please?"

Beulah's eyes widened.

Myles wiped a hand down his face, appearing to consider the request. "Why?"

"I want you to teach me. C'mon, Myles! Beulah's never seen you do it."

She saw his gaze flick toward her, then toward Al. He fired the baseball at Al, who snagged it with a flick of his wrist. "You can walk on your hands? Where'd you learn that trick?"

"I worked for a circus once. The acrobats taught me a thing or two."

Beulah fought to keep her jaw from dropping.

"No kidding? I'd like to see some tricks. Wouldn't you, Beulah?" Al enlisted her support.

Beulah nodded, trying not to appear overly interested.

Myles studied the green sweep of grass. "All right." He removed his hat. "Can't do splits or I'll rip my overalls," he said with a sheepish grin.

"If I tried splits, I'd rip more than that," Al admitted.

Myles upended and walked across the yard on his hands, booted feet dangling above his head. He paused to balance on first one hand, then the other. With a quick jerk, he landed back on his feet, then whirled into a series of front handsprings, ending with a deep bow. His audience cheered and clapped.

"Amazing!" Al said. "I never knew you could do that."

"Your face is red like a tomato," Samuel said.

Beulah met Myles's gaze. Did she imagine it, or did his eyes reveal a desire to please? Heart pounding again, she managed an admiring smile. "Who needs to see a circus when we have Myles?"

He seemed to grow taller; his shoulders squared. "You would enjoy a real circus."

"So let's go!" Samuel persisted. "Beulah, you've gotta help me ask Mama. With Myles and Al taking us, I'm sure she'll say we can go."

"Do you want to take us?" Beulah asked, carefully looking at neither man.

"It might be fun," Al wavered.

"I do." Myles's direct answer took everyone by surprise. "I'm going for the parade and the show."

❦

Beulah and Eunice hurried into the kitchen. Beulah tied her bonnet beneath her chin, setting the bow at the perfect angle. "Does this bonnet match this dress, Mama?"

Violet cast her a quick glance. "It's sweet, Dear."

"Now you stay close; no wandering off by yourself," she warned Samuel while combing back his persistent cowlick. "Being ten does not mean you're grown up." The boy squirmed and contorted his face.

Obie watched them from his seat at the kitchen table, his chest supporting a sleeping baby Daniel. Amusement twitched his thick mustache.

"I'll behave, Mama," Samuel said. "Do you think there will be elephants in the parade, Pa? Maybe bears and lions! Myles used to be in the circus. He says it was lots of work. I think I'd rather be a preacher when I grow up."

His stepfather lifted a brow. "Preachers don't have to work, you figure?"

"Reverend Schoengard doesn't work much. He just drives around visiting people and writes sermons."

Obie chuckled. "Our pastor more than earns his keep. You don't get muscles like his by sitting around all the time."

Eunice was still braiding one long pigtail. "I'm so glad it stopped raining! Now it's all sunny and pretty—the perfect day for a circus. Are they here yet?" She hurried to the window and peered toward the barn.

Obie tipped back his chair and balanced on his toes. "They're hitching the horses to the surrey. Should be ready soon."

"Can I go help, Pa?" Samuel begged.

"Ask your mother."

"You may. Try not to get too dirty." Violet released her restless son. "I'm trusting you to keep your brother in line, girls. Don't get so involved with your friends that you forget to watch Samuel."

"We won't, Mama," Beulah assured her mother. A crease appeared between her brows. "Our friends? I thought just the five of us were going."

Obie grinned. "I imagine half our town will head over to Bolger this afternoon. Circuses don't come around every day."

"Here come Al and Myles!" Eunice announced, bouncing on her toes.

Beulah bent to kiss Daniel's soft cheek. "Bye, Papa and Mama. Take care and enjoy your free day."

Al was less than pleased when Samuel squeezed between him and Beulah on the surrey's front seat. "Can't you sit in the back? It's crowded up here, and I need elbow room."

The boy's face fell. "Can't I drive a little? Papa lets me drive sometimes. The horses know me."

"I'll climb in back," Beulah offered quickly, rising. When she hopped down, one foot tangled in her skirt and she sat down hard in the dirt, legs splayed. Her skirt ballooned, displaying a fluffy white petticoat and pantaloon. Horrified, she clapped her arms down over the billowing fabric and glanced toward Myles. He was loading the picnic basket behind the surrey's rear seat. Had he seen?

"But, Beulah," Al protested. "I wanted to—Are you all right?"

Beulah scrambled to her feet and brushed off her dress, cheeks afire. "I'm fine."

"I'll drive, if you like," Myles said. "I don't mind sitting with Samuel."

Al looked abashed. "I don't either. It doesn't matter, really."

He settled beside the boy and released the brake. "Climb in."

In the surrey's back seat, Eunice had one hand clamped over her mouth. Her shoulders were shaking. She looked up, met Beulah's eyes, and started giggling again. Beulah felt a smile tug at her mouth. Frowning to conceal it, she climbed up beside her sister and smoothed her skirts. "Stop it!" she hissed.

"You looked so funny!" Eunice nearly choked.

Myles hauled himself up to sit on the other side of Eunice. He must have visited the barber that morning. His beard and hair were neatly trimmed. He watched Eunice mop her eyes with a crumpled handkerchief, but made no comment.

Beulah leaned forward. "Are you excited to see a circus again, Myles?"

He looked at her with raised brows. "Guess I am. It's been a long time."

Conversation flagged. While Samuel chattered with Al, the three in the back seat studied passing scenery with unaccustomed interest. Beulah longed to talk with Myles, but about what? Her mind was blank.

After awhile, Myles cleared his throat. "Lots of traffic today."

"Must be for the circus," Al said. "I think I see the Schoengards up ahead."

Samuel's ears pricked. "Scott is here?"

"You're sitting with us, Sam." Beulah leaned forward to remind him.

"I know. I know," he grouched, pushing her hand from his shoulder.

The streets of Bolger were already crowded. People lined the road into town, standing in and around buggies and wagons. Al parked the surrey beside a farm wagon, easing the team into place. "We can see better from up here," he explained, "and we've got shade." He indicated the surrey's canvas top. "Did you bring water, Beulah?"

Samuel stood and waved his arms, shouting. "Here it comes! I see it!"

A roar went up from the crowds, and Beulah clutched her seat. The horses objected to the commotion. Al had his hands full quieting the rearing animals.

"May want to drop back," Myles advised. "Especially if this circus has elephants."

"You all climb out," Al growled. "Don't want Sam to miss the parade."

Beulah climbed down, but Eunice chose to remain in the surrey. "Al needs company," she said. "You three can find us after the parade."

Grabbing Samuel's hand, Beulah tried to find a place with a clear view. "This way," Myles said, waving to her. He found a front row spot for Samuel, and Beulah clutched her brother's shoulders from behind.

Two elephants wearing spangled harnesses led the parade. Pretty women rode on the beasts' thick necks, waving to the audience. A marching band followed, blaring music that nearly drowned out the crowd's cheers. Beulah watched clowns, caged beasts, a strong man, fat lady, a midget, and several bouncing acrobats. Costumed men shouted invitations. "Come and see the circus! Come to the show!"

Beulah clapped and waved, smiling until her cheeks ached. The crowd pressed about her and waves of heat rose from the dusty road, but she was too enthralled to care. Samuel hopped up and down, waving both arms. "It's a real lion, Beulah! Do you see it? And that huge bear! Was it real?"

When the music died away and the last cage disappeared into the dust, Beulah stepped back—right on someone's foot. Hands cupped her elbows; her shoulder bumped into a solid chest. "Oh! I'm so sorry," she gasped.

"We'd better find Al and Eunice," Myles said. His eyes were a dusty olive hue that matched his plaid shirt.

Beulah shivered in the heat. "Yes. Yes, of course." He turned her around and started walking, guiding her with one hand at her elbow. Beulah walked stiffly; she was afraid to wiggle her arm lest he remove his hand.

Samuel capered beside them, turning cartwheels in the trampled grass. "Have you ever seen a bear that big, Myles? And they've got two elephants, not just one. This is the greatest circus! Did you see those men wearing long underwear do back flips? Why don't they wear clothes, Myles?"

Myles chuckled. "Not underwear, Sam. They wear those snug, stretchy clothes to make it easy to move. It's a costume, you could say. There's the surrey." He waved an arm at Al.

Samuel took off running toward the surrey. "Did you see it? Weren't the elephants great, Eunice?" His sister agreed.

Al's smile looked forced. "We could see pretty well from here. Too well for the horses' peace of mind. They don't care for elephants and lions. I'm hungry. Ready to dig into that supper basket?"

❦

Myles followed the Fairfields and Al into the big tent and took a seat at one end of a bench. Ever since the parade, Al had hovered over Beulah like a dog over a bone. Now he made certain she sat at the far end of the bench. Beulah looked up at Al just before he sat beside her. Myles lifted a brow. That pout of hers was something to see.

Although Myles knew he was a far from impartial observer, he was certain something had changed between Al and Beulah. True, they had never been a particularly affectionate pair, but they appeared to enjoy an easy camaraderie.

No more. Beulah seemed almost eager to escape Al's company. Her attention wandered when he spoke, and her gaze never followed his tall form. Al's dark eyes brooded, and his laughter sounded strained.

Perhaps they had quarreled. It was too much to hope that their romance had died away completely. Everyone in town knew that Al and Beulah would marry someday. Everyone.

Myles studied the sawdust center ring, arms folded across his chest. There was a tightness in his belly. He tried to rub it away. Not even the familiar sounds and smells of the circus could alleviate his distress.

"Are you hungry again, Myles?" Eunice asked over Samuel's head. "We could buy some popcorn."

He tried to stuff the offending hand in his pocket, then crossed his arms again. "I'm not hungry, but I'll buy you a snack." Rising, he approached a vendor and returned with a sack of buttered popcorn. "Don't know how you can eat again so soon, but here you go." Eunice and Samuel piled into the treat, knocking much of it to the floor in their haste.

"Hey, look. Isn't that Marva Obermeier?" Al pointed across the tent. "If you hurry, you could find a seat with her, Myles. We'll join up with you later."

The well-meaning suggestion was more than Myles could endure. Without a glance at Al or Beulah he turned and left the tent. Stalking around the perimeter of the big top, ducking under guy wires, he made his way toward the living quarters.

Evening shadows stretched long on the trampled grass between tents and wheeled cages. From the shadows of one caravan, a large animal gave a disgruntled rumble.

"You there! Mister, the public is not going back here," an accented voice called from behind him.

Myles froze. It couldn't be! He turned slowly, studying the approaching clown. No mistaking that green wig and the wide orange smile. "Antonio? Antonio Spinelli!"

The clown halted. Myles saw dark eyes searching his face. "Who are you?"

"Myles Trent. I'm the boy you taught how to tumble years ago. You used to call me Red, remember?"

Antonio stepped closer, his giant shoes flopping. "Red? The bambino who feared the heights and the bears?" He held out a hand at waist level then lifted it as high as he could reach, and gave a hearty chuckle. "My, how you grow!"

Myles gripped the clown's hand and clapped his shoulder. "I never expected to see you again, Antonio. You're a sight for sore eyes! How's your wife?"

"Ah, my Gina, she had a baby or two or three, and now she stay in the wagon while the show it goes on. We do well, we five—two boys and a dolly." The proud father beamed. "I teach them all to clown as I did you, Red." He scanned Myles once more. "You looka different with that beard on you face. And your hair not so red anymore. You marry? Have a family?"

Myles shook his head. "No. I've got a girl in mind, but she doesn't know it yet."

Antonio laughed again. "You wait until my act, she is over; then you come and see Gina. Tell us all about your ladylove. Yes?"

Myles nodded. "For a quick visit. I'm here with friends."

"This girl in your mind?" Antonio guessed.

"Yes. Problem is, another fellow has her in mind, too."

Antonio pulled a sober face, ludicrous behind his huge painted grin. "That a problem, yes. Now you must put yourself into the lady's mind, that's what! I must run. You stay." He pointed at Myles's feet.

"I'll wait." Myles nodded.

The little clown hurried toward his entrance. Soon Myles heard laughter and applause from the big top, then screams of delighted horror. The aerialists must be performing. He imagined Beulah watching the spectacle, and his smile faded. *If only I could sit beside her, enjoying the show through her eyes.*

The Spinelli family lived in a tiny red coach parked behind the row of animal cages. Myles had to duck to keep from bashing his head on the ceiling, and his feet felt several sizes too large. The redolence of a recent spicy meal made his eyes water.

Antonio's wife Gina was thrilled to see him, kissing him on both cheeks. She shoved a pile of clothing from a chair and told him to sit, then plied him with biscotti, garlic rolls, and a cup of rather viscous coffee. Myles took one sip and knew he wouldn't sleep all night. It was a pleasure to hear the Spinellis' circus stories, yet he could not completely relax and enjoy their company.

A tiny girl with serious dark eyes claimed his lap and played with his string tie while he talked. "This is our Sophia," Gina explained. "The boys, they are helping with the horses. Such a crowd tonight! Never did I expect it in the middle of nohow."

"Nowhere," Myles mumbled.

"We had a problem with the bear today. Did you hear?"

"Gina." Antonio shook his head. "We are not to speak of this."

She touched her lips with red tinted nails. "Oh, and I was forgotting. You will not think of it." She shook her dark head and changed the subject. "So you work at a farm? You are happy at this farm, Red?" Gina had put on weight over the years, yet she was still an attractive woman.

Myles shifted little Sophia to his other knee. "I am. I hope to acquire land of my own before long and raise a family along with cattle and crops."

Gina nodded. Her mind was elsewhere. "And you were such the performer in those days! Our Mario is much like him, don't you think, Antonio? Such a fine boy you were, and how we missed you when you disappeared. It was that brother who chased you off, no? Never did I care for him, though he was your flesh and blood. What become of that one?"

A tide of bitterness rose in his soul. "Monte is dead." Antonio's intense scrutiny produced an explanation. "He was shot by bandits in Texas. Gambling debts and cattle rustling."

The little clown nodded. He had not yet removed his wig and greasepaint. "And you cannot forgive this brother."

Myles sniffed. "Why should I forgive him? He's dead."

"For your own peace of mind. You have the look of a man carrying a heavy load, Red. It will break you, make you bitter and old while you are young."

Myles made a dismissive movement with one hand and watched his own leg jiggle up and down. "I'm starting over here in Wisconsin. The past is gone, forgotten."

"You have not forgotten; oh, no. Grudges are heavy to carry. The past will haunt you until this burden you give to God. Remember how the good Lord tells us that we are forgiven as we forgive others? Why should God forgive you when you will not forgive your fellowman?"

Myles placed the dark-haired "dolly" on her feet and rose. "I'd better return to my companions. It was a pleasure to see you again, Gina." Gloom settled over his soul.

After Myles made his farewells, Antonio accompanied him back to the midway. Darkness had fallen, making support wires and ground stakes difficult to see. Myles felt the need to make casual conversation. It would not be right to leave his old friend in this dismal way.

"This seems like a successful circus," Myles said, ducking beneath a sagging cable. "Are you satisfied with it?"

Antonio shook his head. "Ever since Mr. Bonacelli, he sell out, things not go so well. Lots of us come from Bonacelli's Circus—some of the animals, even. The new owner, he cut the pay and the feed to make a profit. The animals not so happy anymore."

"Is the bear the one that came at me while I was cleaning his cage?" Myles grimaced at the memory of falling through the cage doorway with hot breath and foam on his heels.

"The very same." Antonio frowned. "He's a bad one, sure. You were right to fear the beast. He only get meaner as he get old. He ripped up our animal trainer we had who liked his corn liquor too well."

"I can believe it. Was it the same bear that made trouble today?"

Antonio glanced around. "Not to speak of this!" he whispered.

"Those cages don't look sturdy. I wouldn't want my little ones playing near them if I were you."

Antonio nodded and pushed Myles toward the main entrance. "Gina keeps the bambinos to home. You not to worry, my friend. Ah, it looks like the show, she is over. You had best find your friends quick. Is this lady with the yellow hair the one who lives in your head?"

Myles glanced up to see Marva Obermeier approaching. "No. She's just a friend." But a moment later Marva was attached to his arm. Myles introduced her to Antonio, attempting to be polite. The clown's eyes twinkled.

"I didn't know you knew any clowns, Myles," Marva chattered in her amiable, mindless way. "Wasn't that a tremendous show? It was so exciting when. . ." Myles tuned her out, scanning the passing crowds.

He spotted Al's broad gray hat. "Al!" Waving his free arm, he gave a sharp whistle and saw his friend's head turn. "Over here!"

Marva was excusing herself. "My papa is beckoning—I must go. It was nice to meet you. . ."

Myles tuned her out again, focusing on Al until he spotted Beulah behind him. "Here she comes—the tall girl in the blue dress. Beulah Fairfield."

Antonio regarded Myles with evident amusement. "Your other lady friend is gone. Did you notice?"

Myles glanced around. Marva had disappeared. "Did I tell her good-bye?"

"You did." Still grinning, Antonio turned to study Beulah.

Myles made his introductions all around. Samuel was thrilled to meet a real clown and plied the man with questions. Antonio answered the boy patiently.

"How long ago did you two know each other?" Beulah asked.

"This fine fellow was but a lad with hair like fire," Antonio said, eyes twinkling.

"It has been about eight years," Myles said. "Antonio and his wife were newly married. Now they have three children."

"Myles tells me he has thoughts of family for himself." Antonio wagged one finger beside his ear. "Time, she is passing him by."

Myles felt his face grow hot.

Al gruffly reminded them that home was still a good drive away. Antonio bade the Fairfields and Al farewell. Beulah held the clown's hand for a moment. "It was so nice to meet an old friend of Myles. His past has been a mystery to us, but now we know you, Mr. Spinelli."

Beulah's smile had its usual effect: Antonio beamed, shaking her hand in both of his. "But mine is the pleasure, Miss Fairfield, to meet such a lovely lady. Red is a mystery to Gina and me always—so secretive and shy! But in him beats a man's heart, I am knowing. He is needing a great love to banish these burdens he carries and fill his life with laughter and music."

Myles knew a sudden urge to hurry the little clown away before his heart's secret was broadcast to the world. Al relieved his distress by hustling Beulah away. "Give them time alone, Beulah. They haven't seen each other in years. We'll meet you at the surrey, Myles."

As soon as they were out of earshot, Antonio shook his head mournfully. "And this Al, your fine friend, is the other whose heart beats for Beulah. For him it is a sad thing, Red. She must be yours."

Myles lowered one brow. "What makes you say that?"

Antonio waved at the starry sky. "I read it in the stars? But maybe the stars, they are in a young lady's eyes." He laughed and patted Myles's arm. "You will have joy, Red. Gina and I, we will remember you and your Beulah in our prayers each night. Remember what I say about forgiveness—I know this from living it, you see. Don't imagine you are alone. Everyone has choices in life. Think of Beulah—you cannot offer her an unforgiving heart. The poison in you would harm her."

The man was like a flea for persistence. Nodding, Myles pretended to ignore the stinging words. "You will write to me? I live in Longtree, the next town over."

"I not write so good, but Gina will do it. Maybe when the season ends, we come to see you and your little wife."

Myles smiled and hugged the smaller man's shoulders. "Thank you, Antonio. You have given me much-needed encouragement."

❦

Buck met the tired travelers in front of the barn and helped unhitch the horses. "Why are you up so late, Papa? Is Mama still awake?" Eunice asked sleepily.

"Mama and Daniel are asleep. Get ready for bed quietly, children. Go on with you now." Buck shooed his flock toward the house. "We've got church in the morning."

"Thank you, Al. Thank you, Myles. It was a wonderful circus," Beulah paused to say. Her eyes reflected the surrey's sidelamps.

"You're welcome," they each replied.

"See you at church," Al called after her. "May I come pick you up?"

Myles jumped. That would be a sign of serious courtship. Hidden in the shadows behind the surrey, he gritted his teeth and braced himself for her reply.

"Thank you for the offer, but no, I'll see you there," Beulah's voice floated back. "Good night."

Al smacked a harness strap over its peg and tugged his hat down over his eyes. Without a word, he led his horse from its stall and saddled up. Myles felt a pang of sympathy for his friend.

Buck finished caring for the team while Myles saddled his mare. "Got a job for you Monday," Buck said.

"What's that?" Myles asked.

"We got two pasture fence posts snapped off; musta been rotted below ground level. I found Mo among our cows. He may be only a yearling, but he's all bull. I propped up the fence well enough to hold him temporarily; but we've got to replace those posts soon."

"I'll run the materials out there," Al promised.

"And I'll fix the fence," Myles said.

three

Let all bitterness, and wrath, and anger, and clamour, and evil speaking, be put away from you, with all malice.
Ephesians 4:31

Clutching a novel under one arm, Beulah peeked into her mother's room. "I'll be at the pond if you need me, Mama."

Bent over the cradle, Violet finished tucking Daniel's blanket around his feet. Straightening, she turned to smile at her daughter. "Enjoy yourself, Honey. Would you bring in green beans for supper tonight? Samuel caught a dozen bluegill this morning, and beans would be just the thing to go with fried fish."

"He's getting to be quite a fisherman," Beulah observed. "Whatever will we do when school starts up and we lose our provider? You're right, beans sound delicious—or they would if I were hungry. Is Papa around, or did he go into town today?"

Violet led the way downstairs. "He went to help Myles repair the fence the bull broke. Which reminds me. . .I know it's asking a lot of you, Dear, but would you be willing to carry water to the men? They're way out at that northwest pasture beyond the stream."

Beulah followed her mother into the parlor. "Of course I will, Mama. I'm going out anyway."

"You're a dear! You might take along some of those cookies you baked."

Beulah felt slightly guilty about her mother's gratitude, since her motive was not entirely altruistic. "That's a good idea. If I hurry, I'll still have time to read a chapter or two."

Violet settled into a chair and picked up her mending.

"Darling, I want you to know that I've noticed your efforts to be cheerful and kind, and so has Papa Obie. You're my precious girl—I want other people to see and appreciate your beautiful spirit along with your pretty face."

"Do you really think I'm pretty, Mama?" Beulah tried to see her reflection in the window. "Everyone says I look like my real father, and he was homely. At least, I remember him as kind of ungainly and bony with big teeth."

"You have your father's coloring and his gorgeous brown eyes. Your teeth may be a bit crooked, yet they are white and healthy. You have matured this past year, and I think you must have noticed that boys find you attractive. Al certainly does."

Beulah looked down at her figure. "I guess so. I wonder why men are attracted by a woman's shape. When you think about it, we're kind of funny looking."

Violet laughed. "Trust you to say something like that! As for me, I'm thankful that men find women attractive and vice versa. It makes life interesting."

"So it isn't wrong for a girl to enjoy looking at a man?"

"Wrong? Of course not," Violet answered absently. "I enjoy looking at my husband."

"When a girl is interested in a man, what is the best way for her to let him know it?" Beulah perched on the edge of the sofa. "A subtle way, I mean. Without actually saying so."

Violet looked at the ceiling, touching her needle to her lips. "Hmm. Subtle. How about meeting his gaze and smiling? A touch on his arm, perhaps. Touching can be hazardous, however. A lady doesn't want to touch a man too much or he will lose respect for her."

Beulah's lower lip protruded and her brows lowered as a certain memory of a clinging blond recurred. Her mother's advice seemed faulty. A shy man like Myles might be different. He might prefer a woman who took the initiative. "How does a lady know if a man returns her interest?"

Violet's lips twitched. "She will know. Most men are straightforward."

"But how will she know for certain? If a man stares at a girl, does that mean he is interested?"

"That depends on the stare." Violet frowned. "Who has been staring at you?"

"It's a respectful gaze. Don't worry." She hopped to her feet. "Thank you, Mama. I'd better hurry before the day is gone."

Although she took a shortcut through a stretch of forest, the trek to the back pasture was more arduous than Beulah had anticipated. She crossed Samuel's log bridge over the brook, then hiked up the steep bank, nearly dropping the water jug once.

"Why did I think this was such a good idea?" she grouched, hoisting the jug on her hip. "I'll be a sweaty mess again before he sees me." Mosquitoes and deerflies hummed around her head, dodging when she slapped at them. Her arms ached until they felt limp, and her feet burned inside her boots.

Through the trees she caught sight of Papa Obie's mustang Jughead and open pastureland beyond him. The horse's patches of white reflected sunshine as he grazed. Wherever Jughead was, Beulah was certain to find Obie nearby.

Sure enough, there were Obie and Myles, ramming a new post into a hole. Both men had removed their shirts; their damp undervests gaped open to reveal sweaty chests. Suspenders held up faded denim trousers, and battered hats shaded their eyes.

"Hello," she greeted, picking her way between stumps. "I brought water and cookies."

"Beulah!" Obie straightened. "You're an angel of mercy. We've needed a drink yet hated to stop before we finished this post." He exchanged a glance with Myles. "Let's take a break." Myles nodded, and the two men sat on nearby stumps.

Wiping his face with a red kerchief, Obie drained the dipper in one long draught. "Thanks."

Beulah's hands trembled as she handed Myles the dipper. Hazel eyes glinted in his dusty face. He, too, poured the water down his throat and wiped his mustache with the back of one hand. "Thank you."

"More?"

Each man accepted two more drinks, and the jug felt much lighter. Then they gobbled up her molasses cookies. "These are delicious, Beulah. . .but then your cookies always are," Obie said.

She peeked at Myles to see if he agreed. "My favorite." He lifted a half-eaten cookie.

Satisfied, she settled upon a low stump near Obie's feet and arranged her skirts. "How much longer must you work in this heat? Is this the last post?"

"Yes. Once we brace this post and attach the crossbeams, we'll be done. Nasty work." Obie shook his head, betraying a former cowboy's natural aversion to fences. "Myles did most of it before I got here. Planned that well, didn't I?" He grinned at the hired man, and Myles acknowledged the teasing with a smile.

"Ready?"

Myles nodded, and the two returned to their work.

Beulah stayed. Myles never spoke to her, but several times she caught his eye and smiled. He did not smile back. Her heart sank. *He is in love with Miss Obermeier! Whatever shall I do?*

"Beulah, would you bring me the hammer?"

She hurried to comply.

"If you would hand me that spike. . ." Obie requested next.

This time she hovered. "May I help?"

"Not now," Obie puffed. "Better stay back."

Myles lifted the rails into place and Obie hammered in the spikes. The hair on the hired man's forearms and chest was sun-bleached. Sweaty hair curling from beneath his hat held auburn glints. His trousers bagged around slim hips.

From this close range Beulah could locate his ribs and shoulder blades. Sinews protruded in his neck and chest as his muscles strained. When Mama was pregnant with Daniel,

Beulah once sneaked a peek at a human anatomy book in the doctor's office. Myles might have posed for the model of muscles and bones, so many of them were visible beneath his skin.

He glanced up; Beulah looked away, too late. Her body already dripped sweat; now she burned on the inside. *What must he think of me, staring at him like a hussy?* She strolled away, fanning her apron up and down. Grasshoppers fled buzzing before her.

When the last rail was in place, Beulah helped the men gather their tools. Obie loaded his saddlebags. "Thanks again, Myles." He swung into Jughead's saddle. A wisp of grass dangled from the gelding's mouth. "Will you see Beulah home, then check on Cyrus Thwaite for me? He hasn't been eating well since his wife died, and I want to make sure he's all right."

"Yes, Sir, I will."

Obie's silvery eyes smiled, and one brow arched. "You two take your time. Behave yourselves."

Now what did he mean by that? Beulah wondered.

Jughead sprang into motion, hurdling brush and stumps in his way. Within moments he had disappeared from view.

Beulah looked at Myles. "Why didn't you bring a horse? I thought cowboys preferred to ride. Or are you really a clown?" she tried to tease.

Wiping one sleeve across his forehead, he clapped on his hat. Every inch of exposed skin glistened red-brown, and his undervest was sopping. Though he was pleasing to behold, Beulah tried to remain upwind.

"First a clown, then a cowboy, now a farmer." One grimy hand began to rub his belly. "No point in making a horse stand around while I work. The boss was in town this morning; he needed a horse."

"Don't forget your shirt." She scooped it up and held it out.

"Thanks." He slung it over his shoulder and picked up her water jug.

He wouldn't even meet her eyes. Beulah's temper rose. "You don't need to escort me home. You must be tired." She picked up her book.

"Let's cut through Mo's pasture."

Not twenty yards down the sloping pasture, placidly chewing his cud, lay Mo. Shading her eyes, Beulah cast a wary glance at the dormant bull. "Is it safe?"

"He knows me." Myles bent to step through the fence rails. "Come on."

She slipped through the fence easily enough, but her skirt caught on a splinter and Myles had to release it. Beulah kept glancing toward Mo. The bull watched them walk across his field. Slowly he began to rise, back end first.

"Myles, he's getting up!" Beulah caught hold of Myles's arm.

He looked down at her hand on his arm, then back at the yearling Jersey.

Clutching his arm, she let Myles direct her steps and kept both eyes on the bull. Mo began to follow them, trotting over the rough ground.

"Any cookies left?" Myles asked.

"Some broken ones. Why?"

"Mo likes sweets. Don't be frightened, Child. He's too small to harm you."

Child!

When the bull approached to within a few yards, it bawled, and Beulah let out a yelp. "Here, give him the cookies!" She shoved the sack into Myles's hands, then cowered behind him. The man's cotton undervest was damp beneath her hands, but the solid feel of him was reassuring. Beulah could hear her own heartbeat.

Myles extended a piece of cookie. "Come and get it, Li'l Mo. You've had your fun, scaring Beulah. Now show her what a good fellow you are."

Shaking his head, the young bull pawed the ground and gave a feinting charge. Myles held his ground. Mo stretched toward the cookie, nostrils twitching. When the bull accepted the treat, Myles took hold of the brass ring in its nose. "Good lad." He stroked Mo's neck and scratched around the animal's ears. "This is one fine little bull."

Beulah began to relax, peeking around Myles's shoulder. "I can't believe he was once a tiny calf. Samuel named him 'Moo-moo.' Remember that day when my mother drove us to your farm—Al's farm—by mistake? Or were you there that day?"

"I was there. I helped deliver this fellow that very morning." With a farewell pat for Mo, Myles turned to Beulah. "I remember how cross you looked that day. You've got a pretty smile, but your pout is like nothing I've ever seen." His grin showed white through his beard.

Beulah gaped, hands dangling. She took a step back and tucked her hands under her elbows. "I—I was not cross; I was worried."

"With your lip sticking out and your eyes stormy, just like now." His hat shaded his face, yet Beulah caught the glint in his eyes.

She covered her mouth with one hand, conscious of her overbite. Eyes burning, she turned and picked up the water jug. If Myles knew how she felt about him, he would laugh, and the whole town would know about Beulah's infatuation within days. Marva would regard her with pity and mild amusement.

"Are you all right, Beulah?" Myles took two steps in her direction. "I didn't mean to hurt your feelings."

"I'm not angry; I'm hot." Water sloshed in the jug. Beulah eyed the sweaty man. "You look hotter." Without pausing for reflection, she dashed the water into his face.

Water dripped from his nose and beard and trickled down his chest. "Did I deserve that?"

He didn't seem angry. A nervous giggle escaped before Beulah could stop it. "You needed a bath."

His eyes flared, and Beulah knew she had better get moving. Picking up her skirts, she dashed for the fence, intending to vanish into the forest. But an arm caught her around the waist. "Not so fast." Without further ceremony he tossed her over his shoulder and picked up the empty jar. Her book flew into the tall grass.

"What are you doing?" she gasped. "Put me down!" He surmounted the fence without apparent difficulty and headed into the woods.

Beulah found it hard to breathe while hanging head down over his shoulder, and her stomach muscles were too weak to lift her upper body for long. In order to draw a good breath she had to put both hands on his back and push herself up. "Myles, a gentleman doesn't treat a lady this way! Please put me down. This is. . .improper," she protested. The grasp of his arm around her legs was disturbing, the solid strength of his shoulder beneath her stomach even more so. There was a roaring in her ears.

"Very well." He hefted her and flung her from him. Beulah fell with splayed arms and horrified expression only to land with a great splash. She had enough presence of mind to shut her mouth before water closed over her head.

Flailing her arms, she managed to right herself, but her face barely cleared the surface when she stood on the rocky bottom. The source of the roaring sound was now clear: The stream poured into this little pool over a lip of rock suspended twelve feet above the surface. The churning water tugged at Beulah's billowing skirts, and bubbles tickled her arms.

"How dare you!" she gasped, sudden fury choking her. "I could have drowned!"

An exaggeration, but the sharpest accusation she could think of at the moment. She had to shout for him to hear her.

Myles stood above her, his boots planted wide, arms folded on his chest. Dapples of sunlight played across his hat and shoulders. "It's not deep," he protested. "I swim here often." His smile was infuriating.

"I can't swim with my boots and clothes on," she blurted, then choked on a mouthful of water. "You. . .you monster! You are no gentleman!"

"I had not observed you behaving like a lady."

"Ooooh!"

Desperate for revenge, she thrashed over to the steep bank and reached for his boots. One frenzied hop and she caught hold around his ankles. No matter how hard she tugged, he remained unmoved. She paused, gasping for air. "Where are we? I've never seen this place."

"Just over half a mile above the beaver pond. The waterfall made this hole, perfect for swimming. It's one of my favorite places on earth."

Beulah tried to look over her shoulder at the lacy waterfall, but her bedraggled sunbonnet blocked her view. Hoping to catch Myles unaware, she gave his feet another sharp jerk, lost her grip, and slid back into the pool. Sputtering with fury, she surfaced again, arms thrashing. Her teeth chattered, although the water was not terribly cold. "Help me out of here!"

He frowned, considering, then removed his hat and boots. After stacking his garments well out of Beulah's reach, he dove into the pool and disappeared.

Beulah let out another little screech, then scanned the pool for him with narrowed eyes. He should pay for this outrage.

He did not come up. Beulah began to feel concerned. Had he hit his head on a rock? "Myles?" she inquired.

"Myles, where are you?" She stepped forward, took a mouthful of water, and coughed. "Myles!" Her hands groped, searching for his body. This pool was too shallow for safe diving. Panic filled her voice. "Myles!"

" 'Ruby lips above the water blowing bubbles soft and fine, but, alas! I was no swimmer, so I lost my Clementine.' " The voice in her ear was a rich baritone.

"Oh!" Beulah's anger revived. "You are dreadful! I thought you had drowned—that's what you wanted me to think!" Even more infuriating was her helpless condition. It was difficult to appear righteously angry when her face barely cleared the surface. Exertion and excitement made her huff for every breath. "How can you be so mean? First you say I'm ugly, then you drop me in the water fully clothed, and then you pretend to drown? And I thought you were a nice person! You're horrible! Cruel!"

"Who said you're ugly?" He caught her by the waist and lifted until her head and shoulders rose out of the water. His hair lay slicked back from his high forehead. She could count the freckles on his peeling nose.

"Let go of me!" The grip of his hands sent her heart into spasms. Her corset's ribs bit into her flesh. She pulled at his fingers, kicking wildly.

He shook her. "If you don't hold still, I'll drop you back in the pool and you can find your own way out."

Her struggles ceased. She gripped his forearms, feeling iron beneath the flesh. *I can't cry! I must keep control.*

"Now who said you were ugly?"

"You did. That was unkind! I can't help having crooked teeth any more than you can help having red hair and freckles!"

He blinked. She saw his eyes focus upon her mouth. She clamped her lips together.

"I never noticed that your teeth are crooked."

"But you said. . ."

"I said I'd never seen a pout like yours. It's like a tornado brewing. Wise people stay out of your way." He grinned. "I would never call you ugly. Your temper, however, deserves that designation, from all I hear."

Beulah gaped into his face.

"Go ahead and flay me alive. I can take it." He smiled.

Her mouth snapped shut. The backs of her eyes burned.

"I've got to put you down for a minute. My arms are giving out." He turned her to face away from him. She placed her hands on top of his at her waist, thankful for her trim figure and sturdy corset.

Hefting her back up, he slowly walked toward the far side of the little pool. As they passed the waterfall, Beulah looked up and felt spray on her face. "Wait!"

Myles stopped, lowering her slightly. Beulah reached out

and touched the sheet of falling water, surprised by its power. "Ohhh, this is wonderful!" Rainbows glimmered in the misty water. She lifted her other hand, straining her upper body toward the falls.

"I can't hold you like this anymore," Myles protested, then let his arms drop.

Startled, Beulah caught hold of his wrists and began to protest; but Myles pulled her back, wrapped his arms around her, and supported her against his body so that her waist was at his chest level. "Go ahead and enjoy the waterfall," he ordered from between her shoulder blades.

Beulah's pounding heart warned her that she had exceeded the bounds of ladylike deportment. "Have you ever walked beneath it?"

"I have." She was sliding down within his grasp.

"Can you walk through it while holding me?" She looked over her shoulder at him and recognized the intimacy of the situation. His arms pressed around her waist and rib cage. He lifted his knee to boost her higher in his grasp.

"Are you—are you sure—are you sure you want me to?"

four

Seek ye the L*ORD* *while he may be found,*
call ye upon him while he is near.
Isaiah 55:6

"Please do!" she begged.

His arms shook both with strain and with excitement. Knowing he should flee temptation, Myles found himself unable to deny Beulah's request. Hopefully she would attribute his strangled voice to physical effort.

Again hefting her higher in his grasp, he walked toward the waterfall, feeling stones turn beneath his feet. Keeping one arm wrapped over his, Beulah lifted her other arm over her head to greet the cascade as it tumbled over their heads. Water filled their ears, noses, and eyes, dragged on their clothing, and toiled to pull them under. When they emerged on the far side, Beulah coughed. Water dribbled from her every feature. She had slipped down within his grasp, her bonnet was gone, and her arm now clung around his neck. Long eyelashes clumped together when she blinked those glorious brown eyes. Her smile lighted up the grotto. "I will never forget this, Myles."

She was a slender girl, yet she felt substantial in his arms, better than anything he had ever imagined. Oh, but she was lovely with her questioning eyes and her lips that seemed to invite his kisses! Her free hand crept up to rest upon his chest; she must feel the tumult within. His breath came in labored gusts.

Shaking, he gripped her forearms and shoved her away. He shook his head to clear it, reflecting that another dunk under the waterfall might benefit him.

"Myles—" she began, then fell silent. Although she was

obliged to cling to his arms to keep from sinking, he felt her withdrawal. Her chin quivered with cold.

God, help me! I love her so, the wild little kitten.

Without another word Myles hoisted her into his arms, this time in the more conventional carrying position, and slogged across to the far shore. When Beulah turned to crawl up the bank, he caught a glimpse of her face. "Beulah?"

Her booted foot slipped and thumped him in the chest. With a soft grunt, he caught hold of her ankles and gave her an extra boost until she could sit on the mossy bank.

Water streamed from every fold of her clothing. Her hair dripped. Her face was crumpled and red. Her woeful eyes turned Myles to mush.

"Are. . .are you all right?" Assorted endearments struggled on his lips; he dared not speak them aloud. He touched her soggy boot, but she jerked it away, staggered to her feet, and rushed off along the bank of the creek.

❦

When Myles emerged from the forest near Fairfield's Folly, Watchful rose from her cool nest beneath the back porch and came to greet him, tail waving. Thankfully she was not a noisy dog. Myles left the jug on the porch and turned to leave, but the kitchen door opened.

"Hello, Myles."

Myles removed his hat as he turned. "Hello, Mrs. Watson."

Violet Watson cradled Daniel against one shoulder, jiggling him up and down. "My, but it's hot today! I happened to see you out the kitchen window." Her blue eyes scanned him. "I see you've been for a swim."

"Yes, Ma'am."

"I must admit, a dip does sound tempting. So Beulah reached you men with the water and cookies?"

"Yes, Ma'am. Please extend my thanks for all of her thoughtfulness."

Violet smiled. "I'll do that. She must still be reading at the pond. That girl does love to read, and she seldom finds time for it these days. I'm afraid I depend greatly on her help around the house. Maybe I need to give her more afternoons off like this."

Myles nodded, feeling dishonest. He knew Beulah had returned home already, for he had followed her wet trail through the forest. She must have sneaked inside. "I enjoy reading, too."

"Really? Do you also enjoy music? Beulah and I are both fond of music, but we have so little opportunity to hear good music around here."

His ears grew warm. "I enjoy music." Realizing that he was rubbing his stomach, he whipped the offending hand behind his back. Violet didn't seem to notice.

She leaned against the doorframe. "I play the piano a little. Obie bought me a lovely instrument for Christmas, you know, but I do not do it justice. Beulah plays better than I do. Do you sing or play an instrument?"

"Yes, Ma'am."

"I'm thinking of planning a music party after harvest, just for our family and a few friends. Might you be willing to join us?"

"I'd be honored, Ma'am." Myles shifted his weight. "I must be going. Have an errand to run."

"Are you going to see Cyrus Thwaite? That poor man has been so lonely since his wife died. I'm certain he doesn't eat well. Let me pack you a sack of cookies for him."

Myles handed over the empty cookie sack. Little Daniel reached for it, trying to bring the strings to his open mouth.

When Violet returned the full sack, she gave Myles a sweet smile. "Good-bye, and thank you."

❦

Myles's mare whinnied as she trotted up the Thwaite drive. "Hello the house!" Myles called. Swinging down in one easy motion, he left his mare's reins hanging. A knock at the door brought no response. Myles entered, feeling mildly concerned. Cyrus seldom left his farm since his wife Hattie died last spring.

Myles scanned the kitchen, taking a quick peek into the pantry. The sacks of flour and sugar he had delivered the week before had not been touched. Only the coffee supply had been depleted. Dirty cups were stacked in the dry sink, but few plates had been used. He set Violet's sack of cookies on the table.

"Cyrus?" he called, quickly inspecting the rest of the untidy house. Stepping outside, Myles felt the relief of fresh air. A breeze had risen, swaying the birches beyond the drive. "Cyrus?" he bellowed, heading for the barn.

There—he heard a reply. From the barn? Myles broke into a jog. Chickens scattered as he approached the barn door. The cow lowed, turning her head to gaze at him. "Why aren't you out at pasture?" Myles left by the barn's back door. "Cyrus, where are you?"

"Here, Boy." Cyrus waved from across the pasture. He appeared to be leaning on the handle of a spade. At his feet lay a gray mound. Two vultures circled overhead, and crows lined the nearby pasture fence. The swaybacked old mule must have keeled over at last. But by the time Myles crossed the field, he realized that the animal had met a violent death. Its body was mauled.

"What happened?"

Cyrus lifted a long face. "You know how he could unlatch doors; he musta let hisself out last night, poor ol' cuss. Myles, I may be crazy, but this looks like a bear's work to me." He lifted a silencing hand. "I know there ain't been a bear in these parts since Hector here was a long-eared foal, but what else could break a full-growed mule's neck like this?"

Myles studied the claw marks on the animal's carcass. "Why would a bear want to kill an old mule? Surely it might have found better eating nearby." A suspicion popped into his mind.

"Mebbe it's sick or wounded or plain cussed mean. Would ya help me bury what's left Hector?" Cyrus looked halfway ashamed to ask. "Cain't jest see m'self leavin' him for the vultures and coyotes. Thought I'd bury him on this here knoll."

Myles nodded and returned to the barn for another spade.

To give Cyrus credit, he worked harder at eighty than many men worked at thirty; but his body lacked the strength to lift heavy loads of dirt. All too soon he was obliged to sit down. "Was a time I could work like you, Boy, but that time is long past." He wiped his forehead with a grimy handkerchief. "I been putting lots of thought into what's to become of this here farm. Hattie wanted to leave it to Obie, but I don't see much point in that. He's already got more land than he can work."

Myles paused for a breather, leaning on his spade. One callused hand absently rubbed his belly. "You might sell it and live in town. Bet you'd enjoy living at Miss Amelia's boardinghouse, eating her good cooking morning and night. Lots of company for you there."

Cyrus looked pensive. "You paint a tempting picture, Myles boy. I reckon I'd like that mighty well, but I can't see myself selling this farm. Hattie and me built it up when we was young, expecting we'd have a passel of younguns. Never did, though. I figure this land is worth more to me than it would be to a stranger. It's played out. We planted it so many years, took all the good right out'n it."

Myles began to dig again. "I hear there're ways a man can put soil right again by planting other things like beans and peas in it. Some scientists claim it'll work."

Cyrus shook his white head. "I'll never see the backside of a plow again. But if you had a mind to buy, I might reconsider selling. I'd rest easy knowing it was in your hands, Myles." His eyes drifted across the weedy pasture to stump-ridden fields beyond.

"If I—" Myles stopped working to stare at his spade. "You'd sell to me?"

"That sounds about like what I said, don't it? This place needs someone who'll put work and love into it. You've done a sight of work hereabouts already, but I know you've been itching to do more, to make the place what it oughta be.

You're a good man, Myles Trent, and I think you're a man God will use—no matter if folks claim you don't believe in Him. I know better."

Myles met the old man's gaze. "How do you know?"

"You're plumb full of questions that demand answers, and you ain't the kind who'll quit before he finds them answers. God promises that a man who seeks Him will find Him, if he searches with all his heart."

Myles shifted his grip on the handle. "I can't buy your place, Cyrus. No money. I've laid a little by each year, but not enough."

Cyrus pondered, deepening the lines on his brow. "Don't know why, but I got this feeling about you and my farm, Myles. I think God has something in mind, though I cain't begin to tell you what it is."

A deep sigh expanded Myles's chest. When he exhaled, his shoulders drooped. "Unless He plans to drop a fortune into my lap, I'll be a hired hand till the day I die."

"You might could marry rich," Cyrus suggested with a wicked grin. "Naw, I don't mean it. You find yourself a good wife and make this place into a proper home again."

Myles quickly began to dig. Cyrus chuckled. "Why is finding a wife such a chore for you young fellers? I just up and asked Hattie to wed me and got us hitched. No fuss and feathers about it, yet we stayed happy together sixty years. Bet there's more'n one lady in town who'd be eager to accept a fine feller like you. Why not chance it? Might want to wash up first; try hair oil and scented soap. Females like such things."

"A man doesn't want to marry just any woman," Myles objected. His thoughts whirled.

Scented soap. Van Huysen's Soap.

Money. His money.

Farm. His farm?

"Why not? One woman is same as another." Cyrus's grin displayed almost toothless gums. "Comely or homely, fleshy or scrawny, they kin all keep a man warm on long winter nights.

Hattie was never what you might call comely, but then I weren't no prize winner myself!" He cackled. "One woman—that's all you need."

When the hole was deep enough, Myles dragged the carcass over and shoved it in. "That should be deep enough to keep varmints from digging ol' Hector up," he said. Cyrus helped him fill in the hole and tamp it.

"Hope that bear took off for foreign parts," Cyrus remarked. "We don't need a killer loose in these woods."

"I'll warn our neighbors about the possibility of a renegade bear. Want to come to supper at Miss Amelia's boardinghouse with me tonight?"

Cyrus's faded eyes brightened. "That'd be fine. You got a buggy?"

"We can hitch my mare to your buggy," Myles said. "I'll talk with Buck about getting you another mule or horse. You can't stay out here alone with no transportation."

❦

On the way to town, Myles's mare tossed her head and tucked her tail whenever he clucked to her. "Cholla takes being hitched to a buggy as an insult," Myles explained when Cyrus commented on the mare's bad mood.

"Is she yours or Obie's?"

"Mine. Caught and tamed her myself out in Wyoming. Not so pretty to look at, prickly like the cactus she's named for, but she's got legs like iron and a big heart." Myles fondly surveyed his mare's spotted gray hide, wispy tail, and unruly mane.

"And a kind eye. You can tell a lot about a horse by its eyes," Cyrus added.

Miss Amelia Sidwell greeted them at her boardinghouse's dining room door. "Pull out a chair and tuck in. Evenin', Myles. You been taking too much sun."

"You're looking pert today, Amelia," Cyrus commented. "Fine feathers make a fine bird."

Miss Amelia appeared to appreciate the compliment, favoring the old man with a smile. Her blue-checked apron did bring out the blue in her eyes. "What brings you to town, Cyrus? Ain't seen you in a spell." Her voice was as deep as a man's.

"Your cooking draws men like hummingbirds to honeysuckle," Myles assured her, straddling his chair. He returned greetings from other diners, most of whom he knew.

A stranger stared at him from across the table. Myles nodded, and the gentleman nodded back, then looked away.

Amelia scoffed. "Hummingbirds, indeed. More like flies to molasses, I'd say." She ladled soup into Cyrus's bowl. "Got more of you blowflies than I kin handle these days. I'm thinkin' of hiring help."

"You, Amelia?" Boswell Martin, the town sheriff, inquired in his wheezy voice. "I can't imagine you finding help that would suit. What female creature ever found favor in your eyes?"

Never pausing in her labors, Amelia snapped back, "Miss Sidwell to you, Boz Martin—and I'll thank you to keep your remarks to yourself. If that's a chaw in your cheek, you'd best get yourself outside and rid of it. I never heard tell of a man eating with tobacco tucked in his cheek, looking like a hulking chipmunk. If you don't beat all!"

The sheriff meekly shoved back his chair and stepped outside while the other diners struggled to hide their mirth. Myles again met the gaze of the dapper gentleman with bushy side-whiskers. The two men shared an amused smile.

"I ain't never seen you before, Mister." Cyrus directed his comment toward the stranger. "You new in town or jest travelin' through?"

"I arrived in town Tuesday," the gentleman replied. "I am George Poole, lately from New York. I have business in this area."

"Welcome to Longtree, Mr. Poole." Cyrus and Myles reached across the table to shake the newcomer's hand. Poole's handshake was firm, his gaze steady.

The sheriff returned to the table and began to shovel food into his mouth.

"Boz?" Cyrus said. "I lost my mule today—looked like a bear's work."

Sheriff Martin gave the old man a skeptical look, still chewing.

Cyrus forestalled the inevitable protest. "I know there ain't been a bear in these parts for twenty years, but I know what I seen. The varmint broke ol' Hector's neck and left huge claw marks. I'm thinking you ought to organize a hunt before the critter tears up more stock."

Martin nodded and spoke around a mouthful of stew. "I'll get right on it."

"Don't talk with your mouth full," Amelia ordered, reaching over the sheriff's shoulder to place a freshly sliced loaf of bread on the table. Within moments the platter was empty. "You lot behave like hogs at a trough," the gratified cook growled.

"Talk of bears puts me in mind. . .that circus left Bolger this morning," one diner said. "I heard rumors they lost an animal in this area. Did you hear anything about it, Sheriff? Last thing we need in these parts is a roaming lion."

This time Boz swallowed before he spoke. "Nope. Ain't heard a thing."

Again Myles recalled his circus friend Gina Spinelli's slip of the tongue about a rogue bear, but he said nothing. Surely a missing circus bear would have been reported to the authorities. Or would it?

Mr. Poole turned his steel blue eyes upon Miss Amelia. "That was a wonderful meal, Madam. The best meal I've eaten in many a year."

Amelia fluttered. "Why, thank you, Mr. Poole. I'm right glad you liked it. I've got apple dumplings and cream in the kitchen."

"May I take my dessert later this evening? I'm afraid I cannot swallow another bite at the moment." He laid his folded napkin beside his empty plate and pushed back his chair. When he stood, the top of his head was on a level with Amelia's eyes.

Work-worn hands smoothed her starched apron. Myles noticed that her gray hair looked softer than usual; she had styled it a new way instead of slicking it back into a knot. "Certainly, Mr. Poole. You let me know when you're ready for your dessert."

Poole excused himself from the table and left the room, apparently oblivious to the stunned silence that followed Amelia's reply. "But, Amelia—" the sheriff protested.

"Not another word from you." She withered him with a glance. "Not a one of you what cain't fit in your dessert when it's offered. A fine gentleman like Mr. Poole isn't used to stuffing his face, so's a body must make allowances." With a sweep of her skirts, Miss Amelia returned to her kitchen.

Sheriff Martin scowled. "That woman's gone plain loco. A few bows and compliments, and even the best of women plumb lose their heads."

"Jealous, Boz? Maybe you'll get further with the lady if you try bowing and complimenting." Old Cyrus chuckled. "Wouldn't hurt to bathe if you're right serious about courting."

Boz's already florid face turned scarlet. "Reckon she'd take notice?"

"A woman likes it when a man takes pains on her account. Amelia likes things clean and neat."

"Clean" and "neat" were two terms Myles would never have applied to the sheriff. He was startled by the concept that Sheriff Martin wished to court Miss Amelia. Not that the man was too old for marriage—Boz hadn't yet turned fifty. But hard-boiled Martin had never struck him as the marrying kind.

Then again, what made any person wish to marry? A craving for love and companionship, he supposed. The longing to be needed, admired, and desired. The urge to produce children to carry on one's name. Myles could appreciate the sheriff's inclination.

"I'm thinkin' on asking her to the church social Friday," Boz growled, shoving food around on his plate. "How you think I oughta go about it, Cy?"

Enjoying his new role, Cyrus sized Boz up, rubbing his grizzled chin. "You need to head for the barber for a shave and trim, then buy yourself new duds. And no tobaccy. Amelia hates the stuff. Might better drop it now than later."

Boz rubbed his plump jowls with one dirty hand, making a raspy noise. He nodded. "I'll do it." Amid raucous ribbing from the other men at the table, the sheriff rose, hitched up his sagging belt, and headed for the door.

"No dessert, Boz?" Amelia stood in the kitchen doorway, a loaded plate in each hand.

"Not tonight. Got business to attend. Thank you for a wondrous fine meal, *Miss Sidwell.*" Boz bowed awkwardly and made his exit.

Shocked by his unaccustomed formality, Amelia stared after him, shrugged, and plopped dumplings in front of two diners. When she served Myles and Cyrus, she fixed Myles with a shrewd eye. "You takin' Marva Obermeier to the church social, Myles? She's counting on it."

The fork stopped halfway to his mouth, then slowly returned to the plate. "Miss Obermeier?" His stomach sank. "Why would she expect that?"

"You'd be knowing better than I," Amelia snapped and headed back to her kitchen.

Myles gave Cyrus a blank look. The old man lifted a brow. "It's all over town, Myles. Didn't you know?"

The dessert lost its appeal. "I think I've only talked to her twice."

"You mean to say you ain't sweet on her?"

"No. I mean—yes, that's what I mean to say; no, I'm not sweet on her. I hardly know the woman."

"I reckon you'll be getting to know her real soon." Cyrus chuckled.

five

Wrath is cruel, and anger is outrageous;
but who is able to stand before envy?
Proverbs 27:4

Cyrus was no prophet, but he came uncomfortably close. And "uncomfortably close" was an apt description of Marva herself. The blond lady was not unattractive; in fact, in her rosy, plump, blond fashion, she was pretty.

"I'm so happy to see you here tonight, Myles. You've been neglecting church lately." She wagged a finger in his face and moved a step closer. "My papa says I should claim you for my partner at charades."

Myles took a step back. "Why is that?"

"He says you're a natural performer. Have you ever been on the stage?" Marva spoke above the noisy crowd, leaning closer.

"In a way," Myles hedged, shifting backward. "Have you?"

Marva chuckled in her throaty way. "I? Not unless you count school recitations. I play piano in church, but that's different. No one looks at me. Are you warm, Myles? Would you like to step outside for a while?" She stepped closer to make herself heard.

"No, no, I'm fine." Myles moved back and bumped into the wall. He cast a desperate glance around, only to spy Beulah across the room. She sipped lemonade from a cup, then laughed at a comment from her companion. Myles felt a pinch in his chest at the sight of Al's broad shoulders and smooth dark hair. So Beulah had come to the social with Al. The romance must have revived.

"Myles?" He heard someone repeating his name and struggled to focus on Marva's blue eyes.

"Myles, are you all right? You look pale all of a sudden."

"Maybe I do need fresh air." He walked to the door, wishing he could bolt. Across the porch and down the steps, between small clusters of talking, laughing people—fresh air at last. He drew a deep breath and lifted his gaze to the evening sky. A few pink stripes still outlined the horizon; stars multiplied above them.

"It's a lovely night, Myles. I'm glad you brought me to see the sunset." Marva spoke at his elbow, linking her arm through his. "Do you want to take a walk?"

Considering his options, he accepted. "Why not?" He started across the yard surrounding the building that served Longtree as both church and schoolhouse.

Marva trotted to keep up. "Slow down, Myles! We're not racing. Wouldn't you like to stroll away from other people where we can talk?"

"The games will start soon. Wouldn't want to miss them." Myles shortened his stride, but maintained a rapid gait.

Marva began to puff. "I had no idea you enjoyed games so much, Myles. Aren't we rather old for such things?"

"You never outgrow having fun. They're having a spelling competition tonight along with charades." Fun was the farthest thing from his mind at the moment. Surviving the evening without a broken heart would be challenge enough.

When they returned to the steps, Myles escorted Marva through the door. A large woman greeted her. "Marva, Darling, you look lovely tonight. I'm sure Myles thinks so!" Without waiting for a response, she rambled on. "I was just saying to Ruby that your recipe for corn fritters is the best I've ever tasted. You add bits of ham to the mix, right?"

While the women discussed cooking, Myles melted into the crowd. "Pardon me. Pardon," he repeated, trying not to be pushy. Arriving at the refreshment table, he reached for a glass of lemonade.

"Hello, Myles." His outstretched hand froze in place as he recognized the pink taffeta dress across the serving table.

Slowly his gaze moved up a slender form to meet eyes like chips of black ice. Beulah held a ladle in one hand, a cup in the other. "Are you having a pleasant evening? Miss Obermeier looks particularly lovely tonight, flushed from the cool night air."

Myles wanted to return a snappy remark about Beulah's equally blooming complexion, but his mouth would not cooperate. Was it her beauty that immobilized him, or was it her chilly stare?

"Would you like two cups of lemonade?"

"One will do. Uh, do you need help? I mean, with serving?" He worked his way around the table until he stood at her side. Was this a good time to apologize for throwing her into the pond?

She studied his face with puzzled eyes. "No, but you could offer to fetch more lemonade. Mrs. Schoengard and my mother are mixing more at the parsonage. We spent half the day squeezing lemons. I never want to do that again. Caroline Schoengard, you know, the pastor's wife?" she added in answer to his blank look.

"Oh. Yes. Are you having a nice time?"

"It's all right. Far more people showed up than were expected. Poor Mrs. Schoengard was distraught until Mama offered to help. Will you get the lemonade for me? This bowl is nearly empty."

"Right away." He thought he heard Marva call his name as he stepped out the back door, but he pretended not to hear. What a joy this evening would be if he could spend it at Beulah's side! How he longed to partner her at games, to share casual conversation and develop a friendship, to have talk circulate town that Myles Trent was sparking Beulah Fairfield.

Violet met him at the parsonage door. "Why, Myles, how nice to see you!"

He doffed his hat. "Beulah sent me to help. Is the lemonade ready? Her bowl is empty."

"Wonderful! Caroline," Violet called back over her shoulder, "people are drinking the lemonade even without ice."

"I haven't heard any complaints," Myles said. "Lemonade is a treat. Just right to wash down the sandwiches and fried chicken."

"Hello, Myles." The pastor's wife appeared in the kitchen doorway, wiping her hands on a towel. "A Chicago friend of my husband shipped the lemons to us. Wasn't that kind? Far more than our family could use." A lock of blond hair clung to Caroline's forehead.

"You must get off your feet for awhile, Caroline," Violet fussed over her pregnant friend.

"I'm fine." Caroline ignored her and led Myles to the kitchen. "Thank you for the help, Myles. We were about to send for someone to carry this kettle."

Myles wrapped his arms beneath the kettle's handles and lifted. Lemonade sloshed against his chest. Violet gasped. "I knew we should have put it into smaller containers. I'm sorry, Myles. That thing is so heavy—"

"It's all right. If you'll open the door. . ." Myles walked through the house, across the dark churchyard, and up the church steps. Violet and Caroline called further thanks after him, but he was concentrating too hard to reply.

Beulah backed away from the serving table while Myles emptied his kettle into the cut glass punch bowl. Only a few drops trickled down the kettle's side to dampen the tablecloth. Several gray seeds swirled at the bottom of the bowl. "There." Myles set the kettle on the floor and brushed at his shirt. Already he felt sticky.

"You've spilled lemonade all down the front of you; but then, you've probably noticed," Beulah remarked.

"I couldn't help it. Did pretty well coming all that way with a full kettle."

Beulah picked up a napkin and rubbed at his spotted sleeve. "Yes, you did. Thank you, Myles." Her gaze moved past him. "Marva is looking for you."

He cast a hunted glance over one shoulder. "Guess I'd better run. If she asks, tell her I got covered in lemonade and decided to go home."

"You mean, for good?" Beulah's eyes were no longer icy. Her hand touched his forearm. What was it about her mouth that made him think of kissing every time she spoke to him? "Won't you come back?"

Myles placed his other hand over hers and squeezed. "By the time I came back, the party would be about over. It's all right. I'm no socialite anyway. Never have been."

Someone asked for a cup of lemonade. Beulah poured it with shaking hands while Myles admired the downy curve of her neck. The pastor stood up to announce the start of the spelling match, and the milling crowd began to shuffle.

"If you leave, how will Marva get home?" Beulah asked beneath the buzz of conversation. He bent to listen, and her breath tickled his ear. His hand cupped her elbow. Did he imagine it, or did she lean toward him?

"The same way she came, I guess. Why?"

Beulah bit her lip, studying his face. Myles swallowed hard. Suddenly she bent over the table to wipe up a spill. Her voice quivered. "People never will learn to clean up after themselves. Thank you for your help tonight."

"My pleasure. And Beulah. . ." His courage expired.

"Yes?" She looked up for an instant, then dropped her gaze and licked her lips.

"Miss Beulah, may I have some lemonade?" Across the table, a little girl smiled up at Beulah, revealing a wide gap between her teeth.

"Certainly! Looks like you've lost another tooth, Fern. Are you competing in the spelling bee tonight?"

"Of course, Miss Beulah. You sure do look pretty. Wish I could put my hair up."

"It won't be too many years until you can. And thank you."

Beulah filled another cup. "You were saying, Myles?" She took hold of his wrist and pulled his hand away from his stomach. He hadn't even realized he was rubbing it again.

Heat rushed into his face. "Nothing important. I'll see you around." He didn't want to sound like an echo of little Fern. Beulah wasn't just pretty, she was beautiful tonight with her gleaming knot of dark hair, satin skin, full red lips, and those eyes that took his breath away. . .but he had no idea how to tell her so without sounding foolish.

She faced him. "Oh. Well, good night." Her lips puckered, suspiciously resembling a pout. A fire kindled in Myles's belly, and his hands closed into fists. The intent to drag her outside and bare his soul, come what may, began to form in his mind.

"Ready for the spelling bee, Beulah?" Al asked, sliding behind the table to join them. "Hey, good to see you here, Myles! I saw Marva a minute ago. Better start making your move; you know, like we talked about." He gave Myles a wink and an elbow to the ribs.

"Oh. Yeah." Myles said.

"Myles is just leaving," Beulah said in a voice like ice cracking. She linked arms with Al. "I've been looking forward to this all day," she cooed, gazing up with limpid eyes.

Al blinked in surprise, then grinned. "Me, too!"

Myles stared, his fists tightening.

"Don't stand there like a stone statue, Myles; go find Marva," Al advised. "You and I have the prettiest gals in town."

Myles skulked out the back door, his heart dragging in the dust. He vaulted to his mare's back and wheeled her toward the street.

"Leaving already, Myles?"

"Sheriff Boz? What are you doing out here?" He reined Cholla to a halt. She champed her bit and pawed at the gravel road.

"Patrolling the town. It's my job."

"Miss Amelia turned you down," he guessed. "I saw her with that New York man tonight."

Boz hooked his thumbs in his sagging gun belt. "Marva turn you down?"

"I've never asked her anything," he grumbled. "Better luck next time, Boz."

"Nothing to do with luck. I been praying for a good wife, and Amelia's the one God showed me." He rubbed his chin. "It'll just take time to convince her."

❦

"But, Beulah, you promised to be my partner!"

"I told you, I've got a headache. Ask Eunice; she's good at charades." Beulah slumped into a chair behind the serving table and rubbed her temples. "You already won the spelling competition. Isn't that enough?"

Al propped big fists on his hips. "How can a headache come on that fast?"

She shot him a sour look. "You expect me to explain a headache? It's all this noise, and I can hardly breathe."

He folded his arms across his chest and stared down at her. "I'd be happy to take you outside. Beulah, the games won't be any fun if you don't play. I'll sit with you until you feel better."

"No! Please leave me alone. I think I'll go over to the parsonage and ask Mrs. Schoengard if I can lie down."

Al helped her to her feet. "I'll walk you there."

He was so considerate that Beulah could not be as uncivil as she felt. As they passed the line of tethered horses and buggies, she looked for Myles's spotted mare. Cholla was gone. "Does Myles really plan to court Marva?" The question could not be restrained.

"I guess so. I. . ." Al gave her a sideward glance. "Why?"

"I wondered why he left so abruptly right after you advised him to 'make his move.' "

One side of Al's mouth twitched. "No matter what the man says, I think he's afraid of women. He's all right with girls like you and Eunice, but a real woman scares him speechless. Maybe I'll give him more advice and see if I can help."

Beulah reared back. "Albert Moore, I'm eighteen now, and I'll have you know that I'm just as much a woman as Marva Obermeier is!"

"Don't you think I know you're a woman? Beulah, that's what I've been trying to talk with you about these past few weeks, but you'll never give me a chance." On the parsonage steps, Al pulled her to a halt and gripped her shoulders.

Beulah flung his hands off. "That was a cruel thing to say, Al," she raged. "Myles doesn't see me as a little girl, even if you do! Leave me alone. I don't want to talk to you tonight."

The door swung open. Violet appeared, pulling on her gloves. "Is the party over? I was just heading that way—Beulah?" She stepped back as Beulah rushed into the house, gripping her head between her hands.

six

Casting all your care upon him; for he careth for you.
1 Peter 5:7

Beulah was in her kitchen garden picking yet another batch of green beans for supper when Al caught up with her late the following afternoon. "I did it." He slapped a pair of leather gloves against his thigh.

"Did what?" Beulah asked coldly, adding two more beans to her basket.

"I finally told Cousin Buck about my mother's letter and my plan to go to California. He's disappointed in me for 'running out on my responsibilities,' as he phrases it. But, Beulah, when *will* be a good time to go back? My parents will die of old age before it's ever a convenient time."

"It is a difficult situation for you," Beulah agreed, trying to forget her grudge and be courteous. "I imagine Papa will calm down and begin to see your side of the situation. Presently he is thinking only of the work involved for him in keeping two farms running. Do you think you might sell off stock?"

"Our Jerseys? Never! We've worked years to build up our herd. Now that we have a silo for storing feed, we can keep our cows producing milk over the winter. This is not the time to cut back."

"But if there is no one to milk the herd, I can't see—"

"Myles will be here to milk them. Now that the creamery has opened, our farms should start pulling a profit instead of barely keeping us out of debt."

"Then this is poor timing for you to leave your farm, Al. It sounds to me as if you need to make serious choices about which is more important to you, your farm or seeing your parents."

"Nonsense," Al said. "After we bring in the crops, one man can keep the farm going over the winter. There's no reason Myles can't keep things rolling until my return. He should be pleased to have a steady job. During the past few winters he's had to cut ice blocks on the lakes or work up north in the logging towns to support himself."

Beulah turned back to her beans. "Papa Obie says Myles has worked hard for three summers and has little to show for it. Papa thinks you and he ought to grant Myles some land to start up his own farm, or at least give him a partnership. I heard him talking about it with Mama." There was a buoyant feeling in her chest when she spoke Myles's name.

A line appeared between Al's thick brows. "I don't like that partnership idea. Myles is a good fellow, hardworking and honest, but the Bible says we should not be unequally yoked together with unbelievers."

"Myles is not a believer?" Her voice was dull, giving no evidence that an ice pick stabbed at her heart.

Al lifted a significant brow. "Buck hopes that in time God will reach Myles's heart, but I haven't seen any change." He reached over to pick himself a ripe tomato. "If Myles wants land of his own, he should homestead somewhere. There is plenty of land for the taking in this country if a man has the ambition to find it for himself. Why should I give him any of mine?"

"I thought you wanted him to stay here and milk your cows. He can hardly homestead for himself while he's doing your work." *Myles cannot leave, not ever!*

"True," Al admitted. "But he has plenty of time; he's not old." He tossed and caught the tomato with one hand.

"You're younger than Myles," Beulah observed.

"Why are you so interested in Myles Trent?" The tomato slipped from his hand and smashed into the dirt. "First last night, and now today."

"What are you talking about?" Her cheeks flamed, but perhaps Al would not see. "I simply think your attitude is selfish. Kindly stop destroying my produce."

For a moment she heard only puffing noises as Al struggled to restrain hasty words. When he spoke again, his voice was humble. "I'm sorry I said that about Myles; he's a good fellow. Beulah, please. . .I didn't come here to argue. I need to talk with you. It's important."

"Al, I've got to go make supper; I've taken far too long picking these beans. Mama must be wondering if I ever plan to come back inside." She moved along the row of vegetables toward the house.

His mouth dropped open. "But, Beulah—" He started trotting along the outside edge of the garden to intercept her. "Honey, I tried to talk with you last night and you put me off. We can't go on like this! I've got something important to ask. Don't you want to hear?"

"Some other time, Al. I'll see you later." With an insincere smile, she darted up the steps.

Staring after her openmouthed, Al suddenly flung his hat to the ground and let out a roar. "That cuts it! I'm not even sure I want to marry you anymore, you. . .you. . .*woman!*"

❦

"So when are you getting married?" Eunice asked, plopping down on Beulah's bed.

"What?" Beulah stopped brushing her hair and stared at her sister.

"Didn't Al ask you to marry him?"

"Whatever gave you that idea? Do you want me to marry Al?"

"If you marry him, he can't go away." Eunice wrapped her arms around her knees and flung her head forward. Her brown hair, several shades lighter than Beulah's, draped over her knees and arms, hiding her face.

Beulah began to braid her hair. "I don't want to marry Al, Eunice." Red-rimmed eyes gazed from the mirror. Lack of sleep was catching up with her.

The girl's head popped up. She stared at Beulah between wavy locks. "That's silly. Everyone knows you're in love with Al. He's been courting you almost since we arrived in Wisconsin."

"I'm not in love with Al, and I don't want him to court me."

Eunice tossed her hair back. Anger sparked in her ice-blue eyes. "You're afraid to go to California, aren't you? I wouldn't be afraid. I'd go anywhere with Al."

"Then you marry him." Beulah smacked her brush down on the dressing table and rose. Her nightdress fluttered around her legs as she paced across the room. "I don't want to marry Al whether he goes or stays, Eunice. He is not the man I love." She rubbed her hands up and down her bare arms. What had happened to her gentle little sister? What had happened to the entire world? Everything seemed strange and mixed-up.

"Then who is? I can't imagine anyone nicer or handsomer than Al. You haven't got a heart, Beulah. I don't think you'll ever get married."

Beulah swallowed the lump in her throat. "I would rather be an old maid than marry a man I don't love. What has gotten into you, Eunice? This isn't like you."

Biting her lips, Eunice sprang from the bed and rushed out of the room. Beulah heard the girl's feet thumping along the hallway.

❦

Beulah lay in bed, staring toward the ceiling. *It's not as if I've never bickered with Eunice before, but this fight was different. What is wrong with me? Why do I hurt so much inside?*

There was a quiet knock at the door. "Come in."

Light streamed from the candlestick in Violet's hand as she peeked into the room. "I've just come from Eunice's room, and she told me of your quarrel. Beulah, do you need to talk?"

Beulah nodded, and a shuddering sob escaped. Rolling over, she buried her face in her pillow and cried out her misery.

Warm hands rubbed her shoulders and stroked her hair.

At last Beulah turned back, mopping her face with a handkerchief. "Oh, Mama, I'm so unhappy."

"I know. Papa and I have been concerned about you."

"I don't know what to do."

"Tell me."

Beulah blew her nose and propped up on one elbow. She thought for a moment. "I don't know where to begin."

"Why not begin with what hurts?"

Beulah bit her lip. "I'm in love, Mama. . .and oh, it hurts so much! He sees me as just a girl—at least, Al says he does. And I think he doesn't respect me anymore because I touched him too much. And Al says he isn't a believer—but I can't believe he could be so nice and good if he isn't."

Violet frowned. "That cannot be true. Al has always proclaimed his faith in Christ, and we have no reason to doubt him."

"Yes, but he says Myles isn't. Mama, do you think he really wants to marry Miss Obermeier?"

Her mother blinked. "Beulah, do you mean to say you're in love with. . .Myles Trent?"

Beulah nodded.

"Oh, my!" Violet's shoulders drooped. "I had no idea. Papa told me. . ."

"Told you what? Don't you like Myles, Mama?"

"Of course I like him. He's a good man. Obie thinks highly of him. It's just that. . ." She couldn't seem to put her thoughts into words.

"He's only about twenty-five, and I'm eighteen now. Oh, Mama, just looking at him sets my soul on fire! I know he isn't handsome like Al, but he's so. . .so. . ."

Violet sighed. "I understand. He has the same masculine appeal as your papa. It's something about these cowboys, I guess. What did you mean by 'touched him too much,' Beulah?" Her voice sharpened.

Beulah studied her wadded handkerchief and confessed the

waterfall story. "He didn't kiss me or anything, Mama, but I wanted him to." Her eyes closed. "Mama, he's so strong and gentle! It was the most wondrous moment of my life. . .and the worst. I can't help thinking about him all the time and wishing he would hold me again."

Violet brushed a hand across her eyes. "Oh, dear. I had no idea. . . What kind of mother am I to let this go on under my nose?" Her hand dropped to her lap and her shoulders squared. "Darling, you know that Myles has told your papa little about his past. It's not that we don't like him, but I fear he may be hiding from the law—you know, under a false name."

Beulah bolted upright. "Mama, how can you say such a thing? Myles has always been honest. Papa and Al trust him. And he is so polite. I know he has an air about him—sort of mysterious and dangerous, I guess—but that doesn't mean he is a criminal!"

The line between Violet's brows deepened. "I don't mean to accuse him, Dearest, but we cannot be too careful with our daughters. You are a beautiful young woman, and it sounds to me as if you tempted Myles almost beyond his strength to resist. If he does intend to marry Marva—which would perhaps be best for all concerned—you need to leave him alone."

"Mama, how can you say it would be best for him to marry Marva? I told you that I love him!" Beulah caught her breath on a sob.

Violet stood up and began to pace across the room. "But Beulah, what about Al? Eunice tells me that you don't want to marry him, but, Darling, he is steady and dependable—he's your friend, and he loves you. I can't help thinking. . .Well, to be perfectly candid, my dear, you have a tendency to be contrary. Are you certain you're not deciding against Al simply because everyone expects you to marry him?"

Beulah wrapped her arms around her knees and glowered. "Mama, Al is my friend, but he is more like an irritating brother than a lover. When we first met he treated me like fine china; then he got used to me and started acting like himself, and, honestly, Mama, he is so immature and annoying! I can think of few prospects worse than facing Al across the breakfast table every morning for the rest of my life."

Violet stared, shaking her head. "Oh, dear," she repeated. "I must talk with Obie. We may have to let Myles go. . .and that would be difficult, what with Al leaving for California soon. How could we find a replacement?"

Beulah scrambled to her knees, clasped her hands, and begged. "Mama, please don't send him away! He has done nothing wrong—it was entirely my fault!" She thumped a fist into her quilt. "And why shouldn't I marry him if I love him? Even if he sinned in the past, he is an honest man now, and he would be a good husband to me."

Violet seemed to wilt. "Beulah, how can you even consider marrying a man who does not love and serve God? I knew you had strayed from the Lord these past few years, but I thought you understood how vital shared faith is to a marriage."

Beulah sat back on her heels and hung her head. "You won't even give Myles a chance, will you, Mama? How can you be so sure he isn't a believer? He doesn't drink or swear or gamble, and there is goodness in his eyes." Resting her head upon her knees, she began to cry again.

Violet sat down and stroked the girl's long braid. "Beulah, I do want to give Myles a chance—he is a fine young man, and I can see why you admire him. I will ask your papa to talk with him about his faith and about his intentions toward you. But in the meantime, I think it would be best if you spent more time with your girlfriends and stayed away from Myles Trent. Not that we will ban him from the house, but. . ."

"Do you mean I have to hide if I see him coming?"

"I simply don't want you to seek him out, Dearest. If he approaches you, be gracious, of course, as I have taught you. Darling, I will be praying for wisdom and guidance—for your papa and me as well as for you."

She bent to kiss Beulah's damp cheek.

seven

Let nothing be done through strife or vainglory;
but in lowliness of mind let each esteem other
better than themselves.
Philippians 2:3

"Thank you for coming, Mrs. Watson. And thank you for bringing Beulah. Maybe soon we'll be working on her wedding quilt." Sybil Oakley waved good-bye from her front porch as Violet clucked her gray mare into a quick trot.

Beulah waved to her friend until trees hid the girl from sight. "It's hard to believe Sybil is getting married." Beulah sighed.

"She has grown up quickly this past year. You know, many women would have flown into a temper if you'd pointed out flaws in their quilts. Sybil accepted your criticism graciously."

Beulah fanned herself. "I wasn't trying to be unkind."

"Neither were you trying to be kind. Darling, you must learn to think before you speak, or you'll chase away all your friends. You're gifted in many ways: beauty, talent, and intelligence. You don't need to point out other people's faults to make yourself look better."

Beulah was silent. The mare's hoofs clopped along the road, sloshing in occasional puddles. Maple and birch trees were beginning to show patches of yellow and red.

"I'm sorry, Mama. I'll apologize to Sybil next time I see her." Her voice was quiet.

"I've noticed that Al doesn't talk to you when he comes over. Did you quarrel with him, too?"

Beulah braced herself for a pothole in the road. "Not exactly. I think he's mad because I won't let him talk mushy to me. He tries to get romantic, and it makes me uncomfortable. He is my friend, and that's it."

"Have you told him how you feel?"

She wrinkled her nose. "No, but if he doesn't catch on by now, he's dumber than I think."

"Don't be unkind," Violet said. "You haven't told him about your infatuation with Myles, have you?"

"Mama, of course not! It's none of his business—and besides, I don't want to make him mad at Myles. I haven't seen Myles since the church social." Beulah felt glum.

"I did hear that he had dinner with the Obermeiers the other night. I hope he settles down with Marva. She needs a good man to love and spoil."

Beulah closed her eyes against a stab of jealousy.

❦

Singing to herself, Beulah wiped off the table. There was a quiet knock at the open kitchen door behind her. "Samuel is outside. He can play until dark," she called.

"Beulah?"

She spun around, putting a sudsy hand to her heart. "Myles?" It came out in a squeak. "I–I thought you were one of Sam's friends come to play. Papa Obie and Mama are at Cyrus Thwaite's house this evening, and Eunice is at a friend's house. It's just the boys and me at home," she babbled. "And the baby is asleep. I haven't seen you in weeks! Did you need to see my papa?"

Behind him, the sky was pink and filmy gray. A bat darted above the fruit trees, and a fox yapped in the forest. "No. I came to see you. I brought this." He held out a book. "Found it in Mo's pasture this morning. You dropped it that day, didn't you?"

That day—only the most important day of Beulah's life. Feeling conscious of her bare feet and loose braid, Beulah wiped her hands on her apron and reached for the book. "Thank you." It smelled warm, like sunshine and wildflowers. The cover was warped and the pages looked wavy.

"It got wet."

"I can still read it." She looked up.

What would Mama do? Shoulders back. Head high. Cool, even tones. Gracious and hospitable. "Will you come in for coffee and cookies?"

His boots shifted on the floorboards. "First I need to. . .to apologize for throwing you in the creek. That's been weighing on my mind. You were right to be angry—my behavior was inexcusable."

Beulah watched his right hand rub circles on his flat stomach. Why did he always do that? It made her want to touch him. *I can't love a man who doesn't serve God. I can't! Gracious and hospitable, that's all.*

"I forgive you. It was my fault, too. I threw water at you first."

"No hard feelings?"

She glanced up. The entreating look in his eyes reminded her of Samuel. "Would I ask a man to carry lemonade for me if I held a grudge against him?"

Myles smiled. "Guess not. Or maybe you knew I'd spill it all over myself and wanted to get back some of your own."

Beulah opened her mouth to protest, but Myles laughed. "I'm teasing. You're easy to provoke."

Warmth filled Beulah's heart and her cheeks. "So they say. I'm trying to improve. I wish you would smile and laugh more often. Your laugh makes me want to laugh. Now will you come in for coffee and cookies?"

His eyes twinkled. "Thank you. I will."

She lowered her chin and one brow. "What's so funny?"

"You. I'm glad you're back to normal. Those elegant manners make me nervous."

Beulah laughed outright. Forgetting her resolve to be aloof, she grabbed him by a shirt button and dragged him into the kitchen. Planting a hand on his chest, she shoved him into a chair. "Sit. Stay."

He seized her wrist in a lightning motion. "Bossy woman.

If you request, I am your humble servant. If you order. . ." He shook his head. "Another dunk in the creek might be imminent."

"You use awfully big words for a hired hand." Beulah tugged at her arm. "Is that a threat?"

"A warning."

"I guess your apology wasn't genuine." She pouted, thinking how nice it would be to slip into his lap. He smelled of soap and hair oil. "Don't you want to be friends?"

Pressure on her arm brought her closer. "Is that what you want from me?" The low question set her heart hammering. His face was mere inches from hers. Beulah licked her lips.

Scrabbling claws skidded across the floorboards; then Watchful shoved her face and upper body between Beulah and Myles. Panting and wagging, the dog pawed at Myles's chest.

He released Beulah to protect his skin from Watchful's claws. "Down, Girl. I'm glad to see you, too." He forced the dog to the floor, then thumped her sides affectionately. Glancing toward the door, he said, "Hello, Sam."

Samuel stamped his boots on the porch, tossed his hat on a hook, and flopped into a chair. "Howdy, Myles. You come for cookies?"

"Just trying to sweet-talk your sister into giving me some. See if you can influence her."

Beulah propped her fists on her hips. "Not necessary. Samuel, you wash your hands first and bring in the milk, please." She moved to the stove and poured two cups of coffee.

The boy made a face at her back but obeyed.

"Bossy, isn't she?" Myles observed.

"You said it!" Samuel pumped water over his soapy hands, then ran outside to the springhouse.

Beulah's spine stiffened. She set a steaming cup in front of Myles. "Sugar? Milk?"

"Black is fine."

She felt his gaze while she took cookies from the crock and

arranged them on a plate. "I'm not bossy," she hissed.

"Do you prefer 'imperious'?" His eyes crinkled at the corners. "You're rewarding to tease, and you somehow manage to be pretty when you're cross. Unfair to the male of the species, since you seem to be cross much of the time. I have observed, however, that your smile is to your frown what a clear sunrise is to a misty morning. Each wields its charm, yet one is far more appealing than the other."

Confounded by this speech, Beulah settled across from him. She was pondering an answer when Samuel clattered up the steps, carrying the milk. "Save some for me," he protested, seeing Myles pop an entire cookie into his mouth.

Still chewing, Myles wrapped his forearms around the plate of cookies and gave Samuel a provoking smile. "Mine."

Samuel pitched into him. Myles caught the boy's arms and held him off easily, but Samuel was a determined opponent. Beulah watched helplessly as they wrestled at the table. She rescued Myles's coffee just in time. "Boys, behave yourselves!"

The chair tipped over, and Myles landed on the floor, laughing. "Truce," he gasped. "I'll share."

Samuel was equally breathless and merry. "I beat you," he claimed. He thumped Myles in the stomach, and the man's knees came up with a jerk.

"Samuel! Don't be mean!" Beulah jumped to her feet. "Are you all right, Myles?"

Samuel gave her a scornful glare. "Don't be silly. I couldn't hurt him."

Myles sat up, resting an arm on his upended chair. "Aw, let her protect me if she wants to. I like it." Rubbing his belly, he smiled up at Beulah, and she felt her face grow warm.

Myles and Samuel talked baseball and fishing while they finished off the cookies. Sipping her coffee, Beulah listened, watching their animated faces and smiling at their quips and gibes.

"So where's Al?" Samuel looked at Beulah, then at Myles.

Beulah collected the empty dishes and carried them to the sink. Leaning back in the chair with an ankle resting on his knee, Myles stroked his beard. "Reckon he's at home."

"Why didn't he come with you?"

"He didn't know I was coming."

"He was here last night," Samuel said. "Eunice and I played marbles with him. Do you want to come play catch with me tomorrow?"

"Just might do that. Better enjoy free time while we have it. Harvest starts in a few days, and from then on, we work like slaves." Myles rose and stretched his arms. "Guess I'd better get on back."

"Bye, Myles." Samuel left the room without ceremony.

Taking his hat from the table, Myles twisted it between his hands. "Thank you for the cookies and the good company, Beulah. Can't remember when I've had a nicer evening."

"I can't either." Beulah clasped her hands behind her. "I'm glad you came over." She backed away, giving him room to pass.

His eyes searched her face. "So am I." He clapped on his hat and disappeared into the night.

eight

He healeth the broken in heart,
and bindeth up their wounds.
Psalm 147:3

Rapid footfalls approached the main barn from outside. "Myles? Al? Is anyone here?" Beulah called.

"I'm here," Myles answered. He set aside the broken stall door and rose, brushing wood shavings from his hands. "Al is out. Do you need him?"

Beulah stopped in the barn doorway, eyes wide, chest heaving. "I. . .well. . ." She hopped from one foot to the other, her gaze shifting about the barn. "Oh, what can it hurt? I need your help! Please come quickly, Myles."

"Are you ill? Hurt? Come, sit down here." He indicated the bench.

"No, no, I need help," she panted. "I found a cat caught by a fishhook down near the beaver dam. Do you have something I can use to cut it loose?"

A cat? Myles put his hammer into his neat toolbox and selected a pair of pliers. After plucking his hat from a hook on the barn wall, he pulled it low over his forehead. "Lead on."

"I hope I can find the cat again." Beulah was beginning to catch her breath. Her bound braid hung cockeyed on the side of her head; her sunbonnet lay upon her shoulders.

"We'll find it." He followed her outside into blinding sunlight.

She pulled her sunbonnet back into place and retied the strings. "Do you like cats? I've never been fond of them, but this one purred when I touched it. Even if it hissed at me, I still couldn't leave it to die. Could you?"

"Of course not." Myles frowned, seized by a premonition.

When they entered the forest Beulah took the lead. Myles followed her slim form through the trees, keeping close behind her. He heard the cat wailing before they crossed the dam.

"Lucky you heard her instead of some hungry animal." Myles pulled aside branches. Sure enough, there was a familiar round face with the white blotch on the nose. Sorrow and horror formed a lump in his throat. "Hello, Girl. How long have you been here?" He snipped away a tangle of line until only a short piece dangled from the cat's mouth. Slipping one hand beneath her, he lifted Pushy free of the brush and cradled her in his arms. That rumbling purr sounded again, and the cat closed her golden eyes. Myles rubbed behind her ear with one finger, and she pushed her head into his chest. Dried blood caked the white bib beneath the cat's swollen chin. She made a little chirruping noise, her usual greeting.

He felt movement within her body, and the lump in his throat grew, making it difficult to speak. "I think she's expecting kittens."

"Really?" Beulah breathed out the word. "Can you help her, Myles?" She stroked the cat's side, then let her hand rest on Myles's arm.

"I'll try. Let's take her home."

Back in the barn's tack room, he dug with one hand through a box of medical supplies until he found a bottle of ointment. "Please find a blanket to wrap her in."

Beulah returned empty-handed. "The only blankets I can find are stiff with horse sweat and covered in hair. Will my apron do?" she asked, untying it.

He wrapped the cat in Beulah's calico apron, securing its legs against its body so that it could neither scratch nor squirm. Pushy let out a protesting howl, but relaxed and began to purr when he rubbed her head.

Beulah looked amazed. "This is the friendliest cat I have ever seen!"

Myles gave her a quick smile. "She's a special one. She

won't stay wrapped up long, so we've got to work quickly. You hold her head up and her body down while I cut off the end of the hook."

Beulah did as she was told and watched him work. The cat struggled when Myles had to dig for the hook's barb, which protruded beneath her chin. Then *snip* and the barb fell upon Beulah's apron.

"Now we must hold her mouth open so I can slip out the rest of the hook." Myles demonstrated how he wanted Beulah to hold the cat under her arm. Once she had the cat in the right position, he pried its mouth open and struggled to grip the hook with the pliers. Pushy squirmed, gagged, and growled. Myles heard claws shredding Beulah's apron. His hat landed upside down on the floor.

"Got it." Myles held aloft the bit of wire and string. "Better get cotton over that wound before. . ."

Too late. Blood and pus oozed from the wound and dripped upon Beulah's lap. Myles snatched a cotton pad from the worktable and pressed it against the cat's chin. "Sorry about that."

Beulah said nothing. Her eyes were closed.

"Beulah? You. . .uh, might want to clean your dress there." He dropped cotton wool on the spot.

"I—I'm not very good around blood," she whispered.

Myles snatched the cat from her lap and pushed Beulah's head down toward her knees. "Lower your head until the faintness passes."

The apron dropped to the floor. Pushy struggled, trying to right herself. Her claws raked across his chest. "Yeow!" Myles tucked her under his arm, and she relaxed. "Stupid cat."

"Do you think she will live?" Beulah's voice was muffled.

"I hope so. Although I'm sorry about your dress, it's a good thing all that mess came out of her jaw. I'll put ointment on her face and hope her body can heal what we can't help."

"I've been praying for her." Beulah lifted her head. Her face had regained color. She took the jar of ointment and removed the lid.

"Have you? Good."

"Do you believe in God, Myles?" Beulah held out the jar.

"I believe there is a God."

She smiled. "I thought you must. Al said you weren't a believer."

He found it hard to meet her gaze. "Al can't be blamed for that. I guess I've been fighting God. Painful things happened in my past, and I blamed Him." Myles dipped a finger into the ointment. "I've had a lot of talks with Buck—Obie—about God."

"I know who you mean. All of Papa's old friends call him Buck—it's his middle name. So you don't blame God now?"

Myles evaded the question. "It isn't logical to blame God for the evil in the world."

"Feelings are seldom logical," Beulah said.

His hands paused. "True. Which is why it's dangerous to live by one's feelings." Myles held Pushy's head still as he smoothed ointment over her chin. She resumed her cheery purr.

"Pushy here must wonder why I am hurting her, yet she trusts me. This simple cat has greater faith than I do." There was a catch in his voice.

"She is your cat, Myles?"

"She lives in our barn. I named her Pushy because she finds ways to get me to pet her and feed her. I realize now that I hadn't seen her around for days, yet I didn't think to search for her." He fixed his eyes upon Pushy, trying to hide his face from Beulah. She would think he was foolish to become emotional over a cat. Pushy closed her eyes and savored his gentle rubbing.

So lightly that he scarcely felt it, Beulah skimmed his hair with her fingers. "You can't be everywhere and think of everything the way God does, Myles. I'm sure Pushy forgives you. You didn't intend to let her down. It was a human mistake."

"We humans make a lot of mistakes." Bitterness laced his voice.

"My mother says that's why we need to be patient with each other." She sighed. "People can be so annoying, and my first reaction is to say something nasty. My mother says it's because I'm proud and think myself better than other people."

Myles lifted his head until he could feel Beulah's touch. "Do you?"

"Think myself better? Sometimes I do," she said so softly he could hardly hear. Her fingers threaded through his hair. "Deep inside I know I'm not better, though. I don't like being mean."

Her touch made it difficult to concentrate. Myles closed his eyes. "You're being nice to me right now. My grandmother used to rub my head like this."

"You look as if you might start purring." Beulah laughed.

Hearing laughter in her voice, he smiled. "P-d-d-r-r-r. I can't do it like Pushy does."

Pushy climbed from his arms into Beulah's lap, tucked in her paws, and settled down to purr. The two humans paid her no attention. Myles shifted his weight and sat close to Beulah's feet. She put both hands to work, rubbing his temples and the nape of his neck. "I've got chills down my spine, this feels so good," he said, letting his head loll against her hands.

"Your hair ranges in shade from auburn to sandy blond."

"Yeah, but it's still red hair."

"Did you used to get teased about it?"

"My nickname was 'Red.'"

"The clown called you that, I remember."

"Antonio and everyone else at the circus. Wish I had dark hair and skin that didn't freckle."

"Like mine?"

"Yours or Al's."

"I used to get teased about my big teeth and about being skinny." She spoke quietly. "I've never told that to anyone but my mother before."

"It hurts, being teased." He reached back and patted her hand.

After massaging his shoulders for a few minutes, she touched the left side of his chest. "Is this your blood or Pushy's?"

Myles looked down, surprised to see a spot of red on his tan shirt. "Mine, I think. She scratched me."

"You had better put ointment on it," Beulah advised. She held out the jar.

Myles unbuttoned three shirt buttons, then his undervest and glanced inside. "It's nothing." He covered it up.

"Let me see."

"Yes, Mother." Feeling sheepish, he exposed the triple scratch, which was reddened and puffy. "I thought you couldn't bear the sight of blood."

"Turn this way." Beulah leaned over the sleeping cat and wiped a fingerful of ointment into the wound until his chest hair lay smeared and flattened across the scratches. "I've never done this before." She pursed her lips in concentration. Myles tried to swallow, but his mouth was too dry.

She looked up and smiled. "There, that should feel better soon." The smile faded. "Did I hurt you? I tried to be gentle. Those scratches are deep."

"Uh. . .Pushy needs a drink." His voice sounded like gravel in a bucket. "I'll fetch milk from the springhouse." Myles scrambled to his feet and rushed from the barn, shaking his head to clear it. The temptation to haul Beulah into his lap and kiss her had nearly overcome his self-control.

He lifted the bottle of milk from its cold storage in the little man-made pool. Conflicting thoughts raced through his mind. *She doesn't know. She thinks I'm a Christian man like Buck and Al. If she knew me, really knew me, would she trust me, touch me with her dear hands?* Myles shook his head, teeth bared in a grimace. *Antonio said I'm poison—full of bitterness and hatred. I would destroy her, the one I love. God, help me! I don't know what to do!*

He rubbed his face with a trembling hand. *Yes, I do know what I should do. If I were an honorable man, I would tell her to leave me alone, tell her to marry Al and be happy.*

When he returned to the barn, Beulah still sat on the bench with Pushy in her lap. The girl's eyes were enormous in her dirty face, and she was chewing on her lower lip. She opened her mouth, but Myles spoke first. "Sorry I took so long. Let's see if Pushy can drink this."

"She's asleep."

"I imagine she'll wake when she smells the milk. Set her on the floor here." He filled the chipped saucer.

Myles was right. Pushy was desperate for the drink, yet she could not lap with her swollen tongue. She sucked up the milk, making pained little cries all the while.

"I thought you were angry with me when you rushed outside," Beulah said.

"Why would I be angry?" Myles kept his eyes upon the cat.

"I shouldn't have touched you like that; you won't respect me anymore."

He let out an incredulous little huff, smiling without real humor. "Won't respect you? That's unlikely." He stared at a pitchfork, unwilling to grant her access to his chaotic thoughts. *Do you know what your touch does to me? Do you dream about me the way I dream about you? Could you be content, married to a wretched, redheaded hired man? What would you think if you knew my past?*

"Does your stomach hurt?"

Myles snatched his hand from his belly.

"Eunice says you must be hungry a lot because you rub your belly so much."

He felt warm. "Nervous habit."

After several saucers of milk, Pushy made an effort to groom. As soon as she lifted her paw to her mouth she remembered the impossibility of using her tongue, but she wiped the paw over her ear anyway.

"Do you think her kittens will live?"

"I felt one moving while I held her. Unless she eats, she will not have milk enough for them." Squatting, Myles rubbed the back of the cat's neck with one finger, and the purr began to rumble. "I'll chop some meat for her tonight. It will have to be soft and wet. I'll keep her in my room until she is well. Poor Pushy. I think she has wanted to be my pet all this time, but I was too busy to notice how special she is."

"You *are* too busy. I hardly ever see you. I wish you would come by for coffee again some evening. My parents wouldn't mind." Beulah rose and shook out her rumpled apron. "I think even I would enjoy having a cat like this one. She's special."

Rising, Myles watched her fold the stained garment. She looked smaller without that voluminous apron. Her simple calico gown complemented her pretty figure. The sunbonnet hung down her back.

The ache in his soul was more than he could endure. *I'm not an honorable man. Al can't have her! I want Beulah for my wife. Whatever it takes, God. Whatever it takes.*

"Would you like to own Pushy?"

"I'm sure she will be happiest here with you." Beulah smiled. "I don't think my mother would want a cat. We already have one animal in the house, and that is enough. I had better be going home now. No one knows where I am. Take care of Pushy, Myles. . .and thank you for coming to her rescue. You may think I'm bossy, but I think you're wonderful!" Rising on tiptoe, she kissed his face above his beard.

He slipped his arms around that slim waist and pulled her close. Her face rested within the open vee of his shirt; her breath heated his skin.

"Why did you do that?" Myles asked gruffly, his cheek pressed against her head.

"I saw my mother kiss Papa Obie that way not long after we met him." She sounded defensive. "She told me she did it to demonstrate gratitude for his kindness."

"No wonder Buck is besotted with your mother." Eyes closed tight, he spoke into her hair.

"I was trying to show affection." Beulah's arms wriggled free and slid around his waist. "Now I understand why Mama likes it when Papa holds her. It's nice."

When her hands pressed against his back, he released her and stepped away. "Come. I will walk with you as far as the dam."

Beulah looked shaken. Myles could think of nothing to say, so they walked in silence.

"Did I shock you?" she asked meekly.

"No."

Beulah had been walking ahead of him on the narrow path, but now she stopped to face him. "I wish I knew what you were thinking. Sometimes I feel as if you are laughing at me on the inside. I must seem young and naive to you."

"Believe me, I'm not laughing," he said. "Do I seem old and dried up to you?"

"Of course not, but you never seem happy. Even when you smile and laugh, there is sadness in your eyes." She tipped her head to one side and searched his face. "Do you ever wish you could talk with someone about. . .about things? I don't think I really know you, Myles. You're like a carrot—most of you is underground."

His lips twitched at her choice of analogy. Fear of overwhelming her prevented him from revealing even a fraction of his desire to be known and loved. "I'll let you know when the carrot is ready for harvest."

"Now I know you're laughing at me!" Dark eyes accusing yet twinkling, she gave him a little shove and hurried away along the trail. "Good-bye, Myles."

"Beulah?"

She glanced back.

"You can demonstrate gratitude to me anytime you like."

Aghast, she turned and ran into the woods. He chuckled.

nine

Thou openest thine hand,
and satisfiest the desire of every living thing.
Psalm 145:16

Myles found the Bible in the bottom of an old saddlebag, smelling of mildewed leather. A spider had nested on the binding—years ago from the looks of it. The title page bore his name in his brother's hieroglyphic script: "Myles Van Huysen, from his brother Monte, 1875."

His squared fingertip caressed the page. "Monte." Memories assailed him: A childhood filled with Monte's derogatory name-calling and cruel tricks whenever Gram's back was turned. Years of adolescent jealousy and competition. Then Monte showing up at the circus—mocking, yet for once honest about his feelings and plans.

Myles stared vacantly at the saddlebag. In Monte's final days something had happened to change him, to turn him from his reckless ways. Was it the shock of finding himself a hunted man? Was it the realization that someone wanted to kill him? Myles shook his head. Danger had never fazed Montague Van Huysen.

He recalled faces around the campfire, cowboys of assorted sizes and colors squatting to drink scalding coffee before heading out to keep watch over the herd. Monte had smiled, a genuine smile containing no scorn, when he handed over the brown paper parcel. "Happy Birthday. The boys gave you a lariat, so I got you something you didn't want. It took me years to stop running from God; hope you're quicker to find Him."

Now, clutching the Book to his bare chest, Myles closed his eyes. "You were right, Monte. I didn't want it. Nearly tossed it away when I saw what it was. Wish I had. Stupid to carry an old book around with me all these years."

He opened it at random. "Isaiah. Never could make heads or tails of those long-winded prophets." Frowning, he looked at the heavy log beams overhead. "All right, God," he growled, "*if* You exist, explain Yourself to me. Beulah says I'm unhappy. Antonio says I'm carrying a burden of unforgiveness. I don't see how I can be held responsible for the wickedness of other people!"

Rising, Myles began to pace back and forth across the small room, his Bible tucked under one arm, a finger holding his place. "I'm not the one who sinned. First my mother gave up on living and left me to Gram. Then Gram favored Monte and made me work like a slave. Monte never gave me a moment's peace; then he followed me around the country all those years as if he really cared what became of me. It's his fault he got killed—" A surge of emotion choked Myles's voice. Grimacing, he struggled to hold back tears. Vehemently he swore.

Sorrow and loss were incompatible with his anger at Monte. Myles clenched his fists and screwed up his face. "I hated him, God! Do You hear me? I hated him! I'm not sorry he died." A sob wrenched his body. "I hate him for being such a fool as to get himself killed. I hate him for being an outlaw. I hate him for being so kind to me right before he died, just so I would mourn him!" Tears streamed down his face and moistened his beard.

He climbed onto his bed, bringing the Bible with him. Flat on his back with the Book lying open on his chest, he continued, "You tell me to forgive people if I want to be forgiven. Ha! What they did was wrong, God! I can't pretend it wasn't and absolve them from guilt." Self-righteousness colored his voice, yet speaking the words gave him no relief. "They didn't ask to be forgiven. They weren't even sorry. I hope they all burn in hell. What do You think of that?"

He pressed upon his aching stomach and groaned aloud. Antonio's words rang in his head: *"You cannot offer Beulah an unforgiving heart.*" Poison. Hatred. The bitterness was eating him alive from within.

"Can You offer me anything better?" he demanded.

If I want God to explain Himself, I'd better read what He has to say. He's not going to talk to me out loud. As if this Book could answer any real questions.

His finger was still holding a place in Isaiah. Myles opened the Book, rolled over, and focused on a page. " 'Ho, every one that thirsteth, come ye to the waters, and he that hath no money; come ye, buy, and eat; yea, come, buy wine and milk without money and without price,' " he read aloud.

How can he that has no money buy something to eat? His soul was thirsty, but this couldn't be speaking about that kind of thirst. Myles read on: " 'Wherefore do ye spend money for that which is not bread? and your labour for that which satisfieth not? hearken diligently unto me, and eat ye that which is good, and let your soul delight itself in fatness.' "

So maybe it really is talking about feeding the soul. I suppose spending "money for that which is not bread" means trying to fill the emptiness inside with meaningless things. Maybe only God can fill that aching void, the hunger and thirst in my soul.

His gaze drifted down the page. " 'Seek ye the LORD while he may be found, call ye upon him while he is near: Let the wicked forsake his way, and the unrighteous man his thoughts: and let him return unto the LORD, and he will have mercy upon him; and to our God, for he will abundantly pardon.' "

Myles stared into space and brooded. Much though he hated to admit it, his hatred and anger were wicked. He was that unrighteous man who harbored evil thoughts. He was in need of pardon.

He read on: " 'For my thoughts are not your thoughts, neither are your ways my ways, saith the LORD. For as the heavens are higher than the earth, so are My ways higher than your ways, and my thoughts than your thoughts.' "

Myles snapped the book shut, eyes wide. A chill ran down

his spine. There was his answer: God does not need to explain Himself. Period.

Myles suddenly felt presumptuous. Insignificant. Like dust. He tucked the Book under his bed, blew out the lamp, and lay awake until the early hours of morning.

❦

If Buck Watson was surprised when Myles started asking him questions about Scripture, he didn't say so. The two men spoke at irregular intervals, sometimes drawing a simple conversation out over hours.

"There are parts of the Bible I can't understand," Myles said as he raked hay on a newly cut field. He felt small beneath the dome of cloudless blue sky. Trees surrounding the pastures flaunted fall colors, reminding him of the passage of time.

"Such as?" Buck prompted.

The two worked as a team, tossing hay into a wagon. The mule team placidly nibbled on hay stubble. Myles looked at other crews around them, their burned and tanned backs exposed to the autumn sun. "I was always told to obey God's commands and He would take care of me. But the Bible tells many stories about good people who were killed or tortured. I've had bad things happen in my life. Wicked people seem to reign supreme; tornadoes, floods, and droughts come; and God sits back and does nothing. The Bible says God is the Author of good, not of evil. I know He knows everything and doesn't have to explain Himself to us lowly people, but my head still wants to argue the point."

"Man has free will to choose good or evil, and those choices can affect the innocent. The whole earth suffers under the curse of sin, and we all feel its effects. Sometimes God intervenes; sometimes He doesn't."

"But why? If He's all powerful, loving, and holy, why doesn't He prevent evil or crush wicked people?" Myles stabbed too hard, driving his pitchfork into the earth.

Buck considered his answer, brows knitted. "There are things we won't know until we reach eternity. You see, Myles, our faith is based not upon what God does but upon Who He is. God tells us that He is just, loving, merciful. We must take Him at His word and know that He will do what is best. He doesn't explain Himself. He doesn't guarantee prosperity and good health. But He does promise to be with us always, guiding and directing our lives for His purpose. Once you place your faith in Him, you will discover, as I have, that He never fails, never disappoints. He will give you perfect peace if you will accept it." Buck forked hay atop the mound in the wagon bed.

"Peace." Myles studied Buck's face and beheld that perfect peace in action. God's reality in Buck Watson's life could not be denied. There was no other explanation for the man.

Myles lifted his shirttail to wipe his sweating face. Over the course of the day, he had peeled down to an unbuttoned shirt. Buck worked shirtless; his shoulders were tanned like leather beneath his suspender straps. "I do want the kind of peace you have," Myles admitted. "I know I'm a sinner, but I'm not as bad as some people."

"When you stand before God, do you think He will accept the excuse that you weren't as bad as some other guy? What is God's requirement for entrance into heaven?"

"I don't know," Myles grumbled.

"Then I'll tell you: Perfection. No sin. None."

Myles jerked around to face his boss. "But that's impossible. Everybody sins. If that is so, then nobody could go to heaven."

A slow smile curled Buck's mustache. "Exactly. The wages of sin is death, and we are all guilty. Doomed."

Myles shook his head in confusion. "How can you smile about this? You must be wrong."

"No, it's the truth. Look it up for yourself in Romans." Buck's gaze held compassion. "But here is the reason I can smile: God loves us, Myles. He is not willing that any should perish. You see the quandary: God is holy—man is sinful. Sin deserves death—we all deserve death. No one is righteous except God Himself. Do you know John 3:16?"

Myles thought for a moment. "Is that the one about 'God so loved the world'?"

Buck nodded. " 'For God so loved the world, that he gave his only begotten Son, that whosoever believeth in him should not perish, but have everlasting life. For God sent not his Son into the world to condemn the world; but that the world through him might be saved.' "

Myles stared into space. "I think I'm beginning to see. . ."

"I would suggest that you start reading the book of Matthew. Read about Jesus, His life and purpose. He is God in the flesh, come to save us. Ask God to make it clear to you."

Myles climbed atop the pile in the wagon, arranging and packing the hay. His brow wrinkled in thought.

"Jesus died in your place, Myles, so you could go to heaven," Buck shouted up to him. "He loves you."

To Myles's irritation, tears burned his eyes. He turned his back on Buck and worked in silence. His work complete, Myles jumped down and leaned against the wagon wheel. A muscle twitched in his cheek, and his body remained taut. "I still have questions."

Gray eyes regarded him with deep understanding. "Nothing wrong with that. God wants you to come to Him with your questions."

Myles glanced at his friend and drew a deep breath. "Buck, I haven't forgotten your past. I don't know how you continued to trust God all those years, especially while you were in prison through no fault of your own."

"I had my ups and downs," Buck said. "Times of despair, times of joy. But I clung to God's promise to bring good out of my life. Sometimes that promise was the only thing I had left."

"But didn't you hate the men who did it to you? I mean, they're all dead now. You've had your revenge. Although I never understood why you went and tried to lead that rat Houghton to God before he died. I should think you would *want* him to rot in hell!"

Buck stopped working and studied Myles. "Hmm. I see." He

rested both hands atop the rake's handle. "I tried hating, Myles. For months, I hated and brooded in that prison, vowing revenge on the lying scum who put me there. Then a friend read me a parable Jesus told about forgiveness; you can find it in the book of Matthew, chapter eighteen. That story changed my life."

Myles grunted. Forgiveness again. He didn't want to hear it.

Buck took a deep breath. "Myles, it comes down to one question: Are you willing to make Jesus your Lord or not?"

Myles stared at a distant haystack and brushed away a persistent fly. There was one thing he could do to make his past right. "I must return to New York."

Buck lifted one brow. "Oh?"

"I'll never have peace until I let my grandmother know where I am and apologize for running away. I can't bring my brother back for her, but I can give her myself. This is something I know God wants me to do." Myles slipped a hand inside his open shirt and scratched his shoulder. "Maybe I should write a letter. If I go back, I might lose everything that's important to me here."

Buck looked into his soul. "Beulah?"

"You know?"

"I'm not blind. Her mother asked me to question your intentions."

Myles swallowed hard. "What about Al?"

"Wrong question. What about Myles? Listen to me, my friend. You can't make your heart right with God. Only Jesus can do that for you."

Myles's head drooped. "I know I'm not good enough for Beulah. A friend told me once that I would poison her with the bitterness in my heart. I've got to work this thing out with God."

Buck crossed his arms, shaking his head sadly. "Until you do, better leave Beulah alone."

Myles lifted his hat and ran one hand back over his sweaty hair. Then he nodded. Climbing into the wagon seat, he loosed the brake, called to the team, and headed for the barn.

Buck moved to a new spot and began to rake.

Al and his crew waited near the barn to unload hay into the loft. After turning his load over to them, Myles watered his team at the huge trough. One mule ducked half its face beneath the water; the other sucked daintily. Myles pushed a layer of surface scum away with one hand, then splashed his face and upper body with the cold water. Much better. He slicked water off his chest with both hands, then plastered back his unruly hair.

Just as he finished hitching the team to an empty wagon, Beulah's voice caught his attention. There she was at the barn, serving cold drinks to the hands. Slim and lovely, dipping water for each man and bestowing her precious smiles. Myles suddenly noticed his raging thirst. Eyes fixed upon Beulah's face, he started across the yard.

Better leave Beulah alone.

Myles halted. Shaking his head, he closed his eyes and rubbed them with his fingers. The woman was like a magnet to him. Buck was right to warn him away from her. *Guess I'll have to do without the drink.* He jogged back to the wagon, leaped to its seat, and slapped the reins on the mules' rumps. "Yah! Get on with you."

"Myles!"

Shading his eyes with one hand, he looked back. Beulah ran behind the jolting wagon, her bonnet upon her shoulders. Water sloshed from the bucket in her hands. "You didn't get your drink. You can't work in this heat without it."

Myles hauled in the mules and wrapped the reins around the brake handle. She hoisted the bucket up to him. Myles took it, holding her gaze. "Thank you." Lifting the dipper several times, he drank his fill.

"Why didn't you come talk to me?" she asked. "I've hardly seen you for days and days. How is Pushy? Any kittens yet?"

"Not yet. She's healing well. She. . .she sleeps between my feet." Myles lost himself in the beauty of Beulah's eyes.

"Myles, are you feeling all right? Maybe you've had too

much sun." Accusation transformed into concern. "Why don't you come inside for awhile. Your face is all red."

Temptation swamped him. What would it hurt to relax for a short time? When Beulah's gaze lowered, he realized that he was rubbing his belly again. She smiled when he began to button his shirt. "Don't bother on my account. You must be roasting." She touched his arm. "Your skin is like fire. Maybe you need another dunk under the waterfall."

Startled, Myles met her teasing gaze. "I washed in the trough. I'll be all right. Buck is waiting for me." His skin did feel scorched where her hand rested on his arm, but it wasn't from sunburn.

The smile faded as her eyes searched his face. "If you're sure. . .Myles, what's wrong?"

"I can't talk with you, Beulah. Not until—You don't even know me, who I really am."

"I know all I need to know. Did my mother tell you not to talk to me?" She sounded angry.

He studied her delicate hand, wondering at its power to thrill or wound him. "No."

"You're still coming to our music party Friday, aren't you?"

"I'll be there." He handed her the bucket. "Better get back to work." Holding her gaze, he tried to smile. "You, too. Lots of thirsty men around here."

She nodded and watched him drive away.

❦

Streams of milk rang inside a metal pail. Al spoke from the next stall. "I've got to leave soon in case we get an early snow. Thanks for all your help preparing this place for winter."

Myles grunted.

"I've given up on marrying Beulah. I don't know why I ever thought she'd make me a good wife. She's pretty, but looks aren't everything. A man wants a woman to be his friend and companion. Beulah flirts one minute and treats me like anathema the next. She about snapped my head off this afternoon. Something was tweaking her tail, that's certain."

Myles chewed his lip. "She hasn't been herself lately. She's got lots of good qualities."

Al snorted. "At the moment I'd be hard-pressed to name one."

"She's your friend. Don't say anything you'll be sorry about later, Al. Just because she isn't meant to be your wife doesn't mean she's not a good woman."

Al grumbled. "I know you're right. But still, I'm thanking the Lord that He prevented me from proposing marriage. What a fix I would be in if she had accepted!"

Myles leaned his head against a tawny flank, fixed his gaze upon the foamy milk in his bucket, and drew a long breath. "I'm thanking Him for the same thing."

"What did you say?"

"I said I'm thanking God that you didn't propose to Beulah."

"Thanks. Say, when did this come about, you talking to God?" Al's grinning face appeared above the stall divider.

"Recently. Been talking to Buck a lot. I've got a past that isn't pretty, but I know I need to make things right. I wrote a letter to my grandmother. Plan to mail it tomorrow when I go to town."

"Will you be able to keep my farm going this winter?"

"Not sure I should make promises at this point, Al."

He sighed. "I guess I understand. Wish I had peace about going to California. I don't feel right about it, and God isn't answering my questions."

As soon as he was alone, Myles allowed a grin to spread across his face. He punched the air in delight, kicked his feet up and stood on his hands, then dropped to his knees. "Thanks, God! I can hardly believe it, but thanks! Soon as I gave in to You and wrote that letter—whizbang! Al is out of the running! Now if I can sell my part of the soap business and buy Cyrus's farm, then. . ."

❦

"Myles, good to see you."

Pausing on the boardwalk in front of the general store,

Myles stared at the speaker. The voice was familiar, but the face? "Sheriff Boz?"

Gone was the tobacco-stained walrus mustache. Looking pounds thinner, Boz Martin sported a crisp white shirt and string tie. The star pinned to his vest sparkled. His gun belt no longer completely disappeared beneath an overhanging paunch. He grinned, showing yellow teeth. Myles had never before seen the man's mouth.

"Don't know me, eh?"

"I haven't seen you at Miss Amelia's in awhile."

"Been staying away. I'm hopin' she'll be surprised, too."

"I'm sure she will be. You look. . .fine."

Boz stood taller, puffing out his chest. "Town's jam-packed with drifters, harvest workers. Lot of riffraff, if you ask me. We had to break up a fight at the Shady Lady last night. You hear about it?"

Myles shook his head.

Boz deflated slightly. "I'll be just as glad when that lot moves on. That New York character, Mr. Poole, left town last week, so I've got hopes Amelia will notice me again. Poole was mighty interested in you, Myles. Can't know why."

"How do you mean, 'interested'?"

"Asked a lot of questions around town. You going to Buck and Violet's party tonight? I can't make it, and neither can Amelia."

"That's too bad. Seems like half the town was invited. The Watsons have a lot of friends."

Peering intently across the street, Boz rose on tiptoe, fingering his gun belt. "That Swedish family south of your place lost a pig a few nights back. Looks like Cyrus's bear ain't left the county after all."

Myles turned to see what was distracting Boz, but saw nothing unusual. "Be glad to help on a hunt. We've been keeping our stock close to the barns, just in case."

"Ain't Al headin' west soon? Hear he's taking Beulah with him."

Myles fingered the letter in his pocket. "Al's catching the train south tomorrow. He's traveling alone."

Boz shifted to one side, frowning past Myles. "That so? Those two make a purty pair."

Blinking in surprise, Myles studied his friend's vacant expression. Another curious glance over his shoulder cleared up the mystery. On the walkway near the livery stable stood Miss Amelia, conversing amiably with the town barber. Myles shook his head and grinned. "Actually, Boz, I'm planning to elope with Beulah tonight after the party. We're moving to Outer Mongolia to open a millinery shop for disgruntled Hottentots."

"Yup. I saw that match coming almost as soon as she stepped off the train."

Myles chuckled. "Never mind. I'll see you later."

Still distracted, Boz waved two fingers. "Later, Myles."

When Myles left the general store, Boz had joined the conversation across the street. Smiling, Myles shifted his bundle under one arm. *Good old Boz. Hope he gets his Amelia.*

The letter was in the mail. Soon Gram would know both where Myles was and what had happened to Monte. *Is that enough, God?*

Cholla dozed at the hitching rail with her eyes half shut. "Howdy, Girl. Bought myself new duds for tonight. Hope you'll recognize me all duded up." The horse rubbed her ears against his hand and lipped his suspender strap. Myles's voice trembled with anticipation. "Think I'll stop at the barber next and get me a shave. Don't know if Beulah likes my beard or not, but I'm through hiding my identity. Maybe tonight I'll tell her about my past. Maybe she'll like the sound of 'Beulah Van Huysen.' "

"Myles!"

He turned on his boot heels. A buxom figure in a calico dress hurried along the boardwalk. Myles stiffened. He wanted to run, but his boots had grown roots.

"Goodness, but it's warm today," Marva panted, waving a

hand before her flushed face. Her eyes were vividly blue. "They say it's going to storm tomorrow, maybe even snow, but I can't believe it! The trees still have most of their leaves. Mr. Watson got his corn in, didn't he? I saw the reaping machine pass our farm yesterday on its way out of town. Papa got our crops in days ago, but then he doesn't farm that much acreage."

She pressed white finger marks into his forearm and shook her head. "You're so brown, Myles, like an Indian! It's not good for fair-skinned people like us to take so much sun. I hope you wear your hat and shirt all the time."

Behind Marva, the Watson buggy stopped at the railing. Samuel and Eunice remained in the buggy while their mother stepped down and tethered her horse.

"Hello, Marva, Dear. So good to see you. Hello, Myles," Violet said in her gracious way.

"I'm looking forward to the party tonight, Mrs. Watson," Marva said as Myles tipped his hat. He tried to smile, but his face felt like dried clay. Marva chattered on, "This will be the social event of the season, I'm certain. I'm inviting Myles to join our family for supper before the party."

Violet gave Myles a look. "How nice! I look forward to seeing your parents, Marva. Is your mother better?"

"Much better, thank you. She and I have practiced a duet, and my papa brought out his fiddle for the occasion. I also look forward to hearing Myles sing. He has a marvelous voice." Marva took Myles by the elbow and pressed close.

Myles attempted to disengage his arm, but she clung tenaciously. Heat rose in his face.

He saw one delicate eyebrow lift as Violet met his gaze. "I, too, anticipate hearing you sing, Myles. Good day to you both."

Without moving away, Marva rattled on as if she had never been interrupted. "I'm sure you must be longing for good home cooking. It's been weeks since you visited us, and my papa keeps asking where you've taken yourself. I told him you've been harvesting for nearly everyone in the county, but he won't be happy 'til you join us for a meal. We can have supper first, then drive to Fairfield's Folly together." The dimple in her right cheek deepened. "What's your favorite pie?"

"Blackbottom. My grandmother used to bake it." Pushing at her hands, he detached himself from her grip. "Miss Obermeier, I really don't—"

"I'll do my best to equal your grandmother's pie. Where are you from, Myles? You seldom speak about yourself." Her gloved hand rested on his chest.

"There's little to speak of." Myles tried to slide the conversation closer to his horse. "Miss Obermeier, I don't think you—"

Marva followed. "Good friends don't use titles, Myles. Please call me Marva. I like to hear you speak my name."

"I must go now. Work doesn't wait for a man." Perhaps it was rude to mount Cholla then and there, but Myles was desperate to escape. Tonight was the night to let Marva know that his heart had already been bestowed elsewhere. His problem was how to communicate any message at all to a woman who never stopped talking.

"Be there at five." Marva rested her hand on his knee in a proprietary way. "Don't forget."

"I'll come after the cows are milked." He spun Cholla around.

Eunice and Samuel waved as Myles passed their buggy. "When's the wedding, Myles?" Eunice teased, and Samuel clasped his hands beside his face and batted his eyes in a fair imitation of Miss Obermeier. Had Myles not been so irritated, he might have been amused.

Glancing over his shoulder, he saw Marva laughing and waving at him. What had gotten into the woman?

Cholla sensed his anger and wrung her tail in distress. As soon as she passed the outskirts of town, Myles let out a "Yah!" Cholla leaped into a full gallop.

ten

Beloved, let us love one another: for love is of God; and everyone that loveth is born of God, and knoweth God.
1 John 4:7

Miss Obermeier finished playing a hymn. A patter of applause trickled through the room as she returned to her seat between Myles and her mother. She leaned over to whisper to Myles. He inclined his head to listen. Marva's pale hair gleamed, and her fair skin contrasted with Myles's ruddy tan.

"Wonder why Myles didn't wear his new duds," Al muttered as Cyrus Thwaite began a mouth organ solo of "Camptown Races."

Beulah met Al's gaze. "He bought new clothes?"

He nodded. "Today. A fancy suit, like for a wedding. Told me he had an announcement to make. I'm guessing there will be a wedding soon."

Beulah jerked as if she had been slapped.

"Maybe it didn't fit," Al mused. "Too bad. Marva looks like a queen, and Myles looks like. . .like a farmhand. I've got to help the man loosen up."

Eunice leaned around Al, frowning and holding a warning finger to her lips. "Don't be rude!" she whispered.

Beulah took shallow breaths. *I won't look. I cannot bear to see Myles sitting with that woman.* Her heart had started aching the moment she saw Myles hand Miss Obermeier down from a buggy, and the pain grew steadily worse. Marva's parents already seemed to regard Myles as a son-in-law.

He never made me any promises, yet I thought there was something special between us. Maybe he does think of me as a child to be amused.

Biting her lower lip, Beulah smoothed the skirt of her sprigged dimity frock. She had been so proud of this dress with its opulent skirts and tiny waist. Violet had fashioned a ruffled neckline that framed the girl's face, revealing the delicate hollow at the base of her throat and a mere hint of collarbone. Now the white ruffles seemed childish.

Marva's royal blue satin gown showed off her white shoulders. Beulah wondered that Marva could keep her countenance in front of Reverend and Mrs. Schoengard. "I think her dress is improper for an unmarried lady."

Al gave her a wry look. "Trust you to say so."

"Shhhh!" Eunice leaned forward again.

Beulah flounced back in her seat. *I was excited to have Myles come tonight. Now I wish he had stayed home. I wish I had never met the horrible man.*

David and Caroline Schoengard rose to stand beside the piano. Violet settled on the stool and opened her music. "We will sing 'Abide with Me,' " Caroline announced in a trembling voice.

Beulah watched the pastor shape his mouth in funny ways as he sang the low notes. Mrs. Schoengard was now heavily pregnant. Their voices were pleasant, but once in awhile Caroline strained for a high note and fell short.

Al shifted in his seat and tugged at his stiff collar while the Schoengards returned to their seats. "Is it almost over?" he whispered.

The only people present who had not yet performed were Al, Myles, and Obie. Beulah knew her stepfather could not carry a tune. He attended Violet's party to be an appreciative audience, he said. And Al would "rather be dead than warble in front of folks."

"Myles, will you play for us?" Violet requested. "Don't be shy; none of us are music critics."

Myles rose, approached the piano, and turned to face his small audience. Candlelight flickered in his eyes and hair. "I'll play, but I have something to tell all of you afterward."

His gaze came to rest upon Beulah. "Something important."

She sucked in a quick breath, lifting one hand to her throat.

Myles placed the piano stool and seated himself. He drew a deep breath and flexed his fingers, seeking Beulah's gaze. The message she read in his eyes at that moment banished her jealousy and insecurity.

He began to play a lively composition. His hands flew across the keyboard with complete mastery. Broad shoulders squared, heavy boot working the pedal, he looked incongruous, yet perfectly at home. His very posture denoted the virtuoso.

Myles completed the piece with a flourish. "Schubert," he said into the ensuing silence. A murmur stirred the room's stuffy air as people audibly exhaled.

"Wow," Al said.

"That was unbelievable, Myles," Violet said. "Never before in my life have I heard—"

"I had no idea you knew how to play piano," Marva protested. "You always let me play and never said a word!"

"You never asked me," Myles said. "This is what I planned to tell you all tonight. My true name is Myles Trent Van Huysen, and during my childhood I was a concert pianist and singer. At age sixteen I ran away, and many years I have wandered the country seeking purpose for my life. Thanks to Buck Watson, I found that purpose here in Longtree. I apologize for keeping my identity a secret all this time. I was wrong to deceive you. With God's help, I am doing my best to make reparation to those I have wronged."

Obie and Al approached Myles with outstretched hands. Beulah watched the men clap Myles on the shoulders and embrace him, expressing forgiveness and acceptance. Soon everyone had gathered around the piano, eager to greet this new Myles.

Beulah joined the crowd, trying to appear happy. What did this mean? Was Myles planning to leave town and return to his concert career? He suddenly seemed far away and beyond her.

"Sing for us, Myles," Violet pleaded.

"Yes, please do," other voices chimed in.

"A love song," Marva requested.

"A love song." Myles appeared at ease in his new role of entertainer. . .but then, the role was not new to him. Acrobat, pianist, singer—what other surprises did the man hold in store? Was there anything he could not do?

Beulah recognized the tune he began to play, but never before had she heard such elegance in the old, familiar words. Myles affected a Scot's accent that would fool any but a native. His voice was smooth, richer than butter.

"O, my love's like a red, red rose,
That's newly sprung in June."

Beulah felt herself blush rose red when Myles caught and held her gaze.

"As fair art thou, my bonnie lass,
So deep in love am I,
And I will love thee still, my dear,
Till a' the seas gang dry."

He was singing the love song to her! Beulah gripped the piano case with both hands, feeling the music reverberate in her soul.

"And fare thee weel, my only love,
And fare thee weel a while!
And I will come again, my love,
Tho' it were ten thousand mile!"

The song ended. Myles lowered his gaze to the keys, releasing Beulah from his spell. "Hope you like Robbie Burns," he spoke into a profound silence. "It was the only love song I could think of at the moment. I know some opera, but didn't think you'd care to hear me sing in Italian."

Beulah drew a deep breath; it caught in her throat.

"Never cared much for fancy singing, but that beats all," Al admitted. "I think I'd be pleased to listen for as long as you cared to sing—and in any language you choose."

"How long had it been since you played the piano?" Violet asked.

Myles figured for a moment. "More than nine years. It's a gift, I guess—being able to play any song I hear. I didn't play those pieces flawlessly, of course, but usually I can play and sing almost anything after hearing it once or twice."

"Amazing! I heard no mistakes. Myles, you have thrilled our souls. Thank you for sharing your gift," Violet said. "I hope you know that you are part of our family, whatever your name."

The entire group murmured agreement.

"If anyone is thirsty or hungry," Violet continued, "we have cider and cookies in the kitchen. You are all welcome to stay as long as you like."

Everyone seemed to relax, and conversations began to buzz. Cyrus and Pastor Schoengard asked Myles to play requests, which he obliged. Strains of "My Old Kentucky Home" and "It Is Well with My Soul" accompanied the chatter. Samuel chased another boy into the parlor, laughing and shouting. Their mothers shooed the boys outside.

Beulah drifted toward the kitchen and claimed a cup of homemade cider. The drink felt cold and unyielding in her stomach, so she left her cup on the counter. She wanted to wander outside amid the fruit trees, but the night was cool and her dress was thin. She could retire to her room for the night, but that would negate any chance of talking with Myles. Wrapping a shawl around her shoulders, she took refuge on the porch swing.

The front door opened and closed. "May I speak with you?"

Startled, Beulah looked up. Moonlight shimmered on a full skirt and fisted hands. Marva's face was hidden in shadow.

"Yes."

The other woman joined her on the swing, making it creak. A moonbeam touched Marva's beautiful hair and traced silver tear streaks on her face. Muscles tensed in her round forearms as she repeatedly clasped her hands.

"Myles loves you." Marva gulped.

Beulah had no idea what to say. *Dear God, please help me to be kind and good.* She pulled her shawl closer and saw Marva do the same. They would both freeze out here on the swing.

"Are you going to marry Al?" Marva asked.

"No."

"Why not?"

"I don't love him that way."

Marva sighed. "You're so young. Do you have any idea what you want in a husband?"

"I know that I don't want to marry a man who is like a brother to me."

"So you would steal a man from another woman?"

Beulah stiffened. "Of course not! What a—" She nearly choked on her own hasty words. Maybe Marva's insinuation was unkind, but it was the desperate charge of a broken heart. What might Beulah be tempted to say under similar circumstances? She felt sudden sympathy for Marva.

"You already had Al. Why did you try to steal Myles from me?" Tears roughened Marva's voice.

"I didn't know you loved him, Miss Obermeier. I wasn't trying to be cruel to you, honestly!"

Marva covered her face with her hands. "It's not fair! It's just not fair."

Beulah patted Marva's shoulder. "My mother tells me that God is always fair. If He doesn't allow you to marry Myles, then He must have someone better in store. You've got to trust Him, Marva. He doesn't make mistakes."

Marva lowered her hands and sucked in a quivering breath. "You're nothing like I thought you were, Beulah Fairfield. Everyone talks about your sharp tongue and quick temper. They must be jealous. You're really a sweet girl." Her tone was doleful. "No wonder Myles loves you. You're both pretty and nice."

"So are you," Beulah said. "Just now I asked God to help me be kind; it doesn't come naturally to me."

Marva gave a moist chuckle. "Me, neither. I came out here wanting to scratch your eyes out! It's easy for you to talk about God bringing someone better along; but when you get to be twenty-six with not so much as a whisker of a husband in sight, you'll know how I feel. Of course, you're likely to be married and a mother several times over by the time you're my age."

She stood up, leaving Beulah in the swing. "When my parents come outside, will you tell them I'm in the buggy?"

"I'll tell them. Are you sure you're all right, Marva?" She followed the older girl down the steps.

Marva shivered. "I'll recover. Humiliation isn't fatal."

"I don't know. I've come close to dying of it more than once."

Marva reached out and hugged Beulah. "Maybe my heart isn't as broken as I thought it was. I feel better already. Myles is a wonderful man, but he never did seem to care for my cooking, and sometimes when I talked to him I saw his eyes kind of glaze over. Guess I'd better be patient and wait for God's choice instead of hunting down a man for myself."

Beulah found it hard to restrain a giggle, but Marva waved off her efforts. "Go ahead and laugh. I know I'm silly." She grinned. "You know, I once even considered Sheriff Martin as a marriage prospect. I didn't consider him long, but the thought crossed my mind."

"Marva, he's old enough to be your father!"

Marva chuckled. "I know. Oops, here come my parents. You'd better get inside before you freeze. I'll see you at church, Beulah."

❦

"I would take it as a favor if you would sing in church," Reverend David Schoengard said in a hushed voice. "God could mightily use a talent like yours."

"I hope He will," Myles replied. "When the time is right, I will let you know."

"Don't wait too long," David advised.

"I am still learning what it means to honor Jesus as Lord. You know that story about the lost sheep? That's me."

"The church door is open to lost sheep."

A small boy tugged at the pastor's leg. "Dad, Ernie hit me."

"Excuse me a moment, please." David squatted to listen to his son.

Myles scanned the room.

"Looking for Beulah?" Al asked. Leaning one elbow on the piano, he sipped a cup of cider. "She's talking with Marva, I think. I spotted the two of them on the porch swing not long ago. If you need help splitting up a cat fight, call on me."

"How did you—"

"Please, don't ask! Anyone with half an eye could have read the look on your face while you sang to Beulah tonight, old friend. I'm thinking you'd better soon have a serious talk with Buck, or he'll be after you with the shotgun." Al's grin was pure mischief. "I'm also thinking I'll have to miss that train tomorrow. Don't you want me to stand up at your wedding?"

"You're not angry?"

"Naw. When two people are right for each other, it's obvious. And vice versa. Beulah and I blended like horseradish and ice cream. You'll be good for her; she needs someone to keep her in line. You should have seen her writhing in jealousy when you showed up with Marva tonight." Al chuckled. "She must have been dying when I talked about what a handsome couple you and Marva made."

Myles felt his face grow warm. "I intended to tell Marva tonight—"

"I don't think you need to say a word. She knows. Her parents just left. They looked pretty sad."

His shoulders slumped. "They're good people, Al. And Marva's a nice lady. I feel bad about hurting her."

Al shrugged. "Some of us are slow to catch on. I wasn't the quickest hog to the trough, myself. Don't know why I couldn't see the attraction between you and Beulah before now. It sticks out like quills on a porcupine. But there will be another girl for me—one who appreciates my humor and thinks I'm great." He grinned.

Myles had to smile. "You're chock-full of brilliant analogies tonight. Porcupine quills?"

"So are you going to talk with Beulah or not?"

❦

He found Beulah on the porch swing. Watchful lay at her feet. The dog flopped a fluffy tail. "Isn't it too cold for swinging?" Myles asked.

Huddled beneath her shawl, Beulah stared up at him. "I guess it is. I needed a place to think, but I've discovered that the front porch isn't private."

Myles leaned a hip against the railing, gazing out past the barn. His left leg jiggled up and down. "Al told me Marva talked to you."

"She was crying at first, but when she left she was laughing. I like her, Myles. She is funny and nice. I think she could be a friend."

He shifted against the rail. "I was planning to explain to her tonight. About you and me, I mean."

Her voice was too bright. "I enjoyed your singing. I don't understand why you hid your talents for so long."

The comment interrupted his train of thought. "It's a long story."

From somewhere beyond the barn came a commotion. Watchful lifted her head, ears pricked. Myles followed the dog's gaze, but saw nothing. Hackles raised, growling softly, the dog trotted down the steps and headed for the barn. The white tip on her tail was visible after the rest of her disappeared.

"Myles?" Beulah stopped swinging and leaned forward. "What is it?"

Watchful began to bark. Myles had never heard such a noise—the dog sounded frantic, terrified. His ears caught the bawling of cattle, trampling hooves.

"I don't know, but I'm gonna find out."

Running feet approached, and two small figures appeared in the moonlight. Myles heard the boys panting before he could identify Samuel and his buddy, Scott Schoengard. "Myles!" Samuel said, stumbling up the steps. "There is something big in the yearling pen—something that roars!"

eleven

We roar all like bears. . . .
Isaiah 59:11

"I called Watchful, but she won't come. Go save her, Myles! That monster will kill her!" Samuel was sobbing.

Myles threw open the front door. "Buck! Al! Trouble at the barn."

Buck snatched up a lantern and a rifle, tossing another gun to Myles. Al caught up with them halfway across the yard. The yearling pen was ominously quiet except for Watchful's shrill yelps. Leaning against the split rail fence, Buck lifted the lantern. On the far side of the pen, many wide eyes reflected the lamplight. A young cow bawled.

"Watchful, come." The stern command brought the collie to heel, ears flattened, tail between her legs. Every hair on the dog's body stood on end. She still yammered at intervals. "Hush, Watchful." Instant silence. She pressed against Buck's leg and shivered.

Buck unlatched the gate, and the three men stepped into the pen. Myles felt the hair on his nape tingle. A cursory examination of the corral revealed that the invader was gone.

Buck studied the muddy ground with a practiced eye. He pointed out bunches of woolly hair on a fence post along with glutinous streaks of blood. "It was a bear."

Myles counted the cattle. "One yearling missing. The Hereford-cross with the white patch on his left hip."

Al measured a print in the mud with his hand. "That was one big bear. It lifted that steer over the fence."

"We'll track it come morning. I don't follow giant bears into dark forests," Buck said with grim humor.

Al crossed his arms. "That monster could have come after one of the children."

"Sam and Scott were playing near the barn," Myles said. He swallowed a wave of nausea at the sudden mental picture of what might have been. "God must have been protecting them. I'll be ready for the hunt first thing tomorrow, Buck."

"Me, too."

Buck lifted a brow at his cousin. "Don't you have to get ready for your trip, Al? Your train leaves at four o'clock tomorrow afternoon."

Al glowered at the ground. "Might know I'd have to miss the fun. All right. I'll feed and milk in the morning, one last time, so you two can hunt."

Something cracked in the darkness near the gate. Watchful's ears pricked. The men spun around, guns lifted. A ghostly figure drifted closer. "It's me—Beulah."

"What are you doing?" Al snapped. "Don't you know there's a bear out here somewhere?"

Beulah clutched her shawl. "I didn't know until now." Her voice sounded small.

"Back inside, Beulah," Buck ordered. "Your mother will worry."

"I'll escort her." Myles stepped out of the corral.

"No lingering."

"Yes, Sir." Myles had never before heard that protective note in Buck's voice. He followed Beulah toward the kitchen door. She drifted beneath the apple trees, crunching leaves beneath her feet.

"I love all our trees and the beautiful fall color, but now comes the hard part—raking," she said in a quivering falsetto. "Did you like the cider? My mother and I made it from our apples."

Myles touched her arm. "Beulah."

She turned. Her eyes were dark pools in her pale face. "Oh, Myles, you aren't really going to hunt that bear, are you? I'm frightened!"

She cared! "I've hunted bears before. Buck and I will hunt this one down in no time. A few shots and it'll be over."

Her hand fluttered up to rest upon his chest. Myles wrapped his fingers around her upper arm. "Buck told me not to linger, but I must tell you tonight. I love you, Beulah. I want to marry you. I want it more than anything." His voice cracked.

He heard her suck in a quick breath. "Do you know God yet, Myles? Mama and Papa both told me to wait until you gave your life to Him. You said something tonight about making your peace with God's help. Did you mean it?"

"I did. I do. I wrote to my grandmother and apologized for running away. I imagine she will contact me soon, and I expect to make a quick trip to New York to wrap up business affairs." His voice trembled with eagerness. "I'm planning to buy the Thwaite farm, Beulah. For us. You and me. How does that sound?"

He wanted to hold her in his arms, but the rifle in his right hand made that impractical.

Beulah touched his beard with two fingers. "It sounds wonderful. . .but are you sure you want to be a farmer? You can do so many things. I've never known anyone like you."

"I'm sure." He leaned the rifle against the back steps and took Beulah into his arms. "Are you sure you want to marry a farmer?"

She captured his face between her hands and gently kissed his lips. "Please don't go away, Myles. Not ever."

"What?" he mumbled, conscious only of his need for another kiss. Her lips warmed beneath his, and her hands gripped his shoulders. Myles kissed her again and again until the cold, dark world faded away. Nothing existed except Beulah, sweet and pliant in his arms.

The kitchen door opened, catching them in a beam of light. "Beulah, it's time for you to come inside," Violet said.

The couple sprang apart, wide-eyed and breathing hard. Beulah grabbed for her falling shawl and rushed past her mother into the house.

"Myles, I believe you need to talk with Obadiah before you meet with Beulah again."

Myles heard the iron behind Violet's mild tone. Gathering his scattered self-control, he nodded and picked up the rifle. "This is Buck's."

Violet took it from him. "Al is waiting for you out front." She started to close the door then paused. "I know you love my daughter, Myles, and I'm not opposed to the match. But as her mother, I must be careful of her purity."

Guilt swamped him. "I understand. I am sorry, Ma'am. It won't happen again."

"See that it doesn't. Good night, Myles Van Huysen."

❦

Myles stepped into predawn darkness, feeling the chill through his wool coat and gloves. A recent dusting of snow on the ground might make tracking more difficult. Cholla was displeased to see him so early, but she accepted her bit after Myles warmed it in his palm. "We're on a hunt, Girl. Like old times."

Cats waited around Cholla's stall, making noisy petition for milk. "Sorry, friends. No milk this morning." Myles thought of Pushy, still sleeping on his bed, and grinned. These cats would rebel for certain if they knew she got her own saucer of cream each morning and evening.

He tied a scabbard to his saddle and shoved his loaded rifle into it, then packed extra cartridges into his saddlebags. "Hope we're back in time to escort Al to the station." He would miss his young boss and friend.

Cholla broke into a canter, tossing her head and blowing steam. Myles hauled her back to a jog. "Too dark for that pace, my lady. We'll get there soon enough."

Buck waited in the yearling paddock. By the first light of dawn, he studied the bear's spoor. Buck nodded greeting as Myles joined him. "Big bear, like Al said. Amazing claw definition for a blackie. I'd say it was a grizzly if I didn't know better."

"Powerful, whatever it is, to carry off a yearling steer. It obviously has little fear of man."

"Makes my heart sit in my throat to think how the children have walked and ridden about the property at all hours these past weeks. And all the while this monster was afoot."

Myles had been having similar thoughts. "Have you heard the rumors that a bear escaped from the circus? If this is the bear I think it might be, our lives have been in constant danger. That grizzly hated people."

Buck swung into his saddle. His jaw clenched in a grim line. "Whether it is or whether it isn't, our job is to end the creature's life."

The bear's trail was easy to follow; it had dragged the carcass through grass and brush. Less than a mile up the creek, they found the remains of the young Hereford crossbreed. "There lies our next year's winter beef supply," Buck grumbled, still on horseback. "This bear has an eye for a tender steak."

Jughead and Cholla snorted and shied at the strong scent of bear. "Steady, Boy. That bear should be miles from here by now." Buck patted his gelding's neck, but the horse would not be quieted. "I don't like this." Buck exchanged glances with Myles, then studied the surrounding brush and trees. Plenty of hiding places for a bear.

Cholla reared slightly, eyes rolling. "What if it stayed around to eat from the kill again?" Myles asked and hauled his gun from its sheath.

Buck swung his mount around, rifle at the ready. "It could happen. This bear doesn't seem to follow standard bruin behavior. Let's see if he's still around." He gave a whoop.

"That should frighten every critter in the county," Myles chuckled. The laughter froze in his throat. Not twenty yards away, a huge cinnamon-brown form rose out of a patch of mist. The bear's roar was more than Cholla could endure. With a rasping squeal, she reared high, pawing the air. Myles forced her back down, but it was impossible to fire while fighting his horse. The bear made a short charge, then paused to rise up and roar again. Foam dripped from its open jaws.

A rifle cracked, and the bear flinched. Infuriated, it charged at Jughead. The mustang bolted with Buck sawing at his reins and shouting.

Myles brought his rifle around, but Cholla chose that moment to shy sideways into the trees. The shot went wild, and Myles lost a stirrup. Furious and frustrated, he decided to let the screaming horse loose and try his chances on foot. He leaped to the ground, and while the bear made a short dash toward Cholla, Myles fired. In his haste, he hit the hump on its back.

Instantly the bear spun around, spotted Myles, and charged with incredible speed. Myles caught a glimpse of flaming eyes, yellow tusks, and a red tongue. Without a thought he cartwheeled to one side, made a front roll, and propelled himself upward to catch hold of a tree branch. He swung his legs up as the bear charged beneath him, still roaring.

All well and good, but now his rifle lay on the ground. "Buck, I'm up a tree!" Could he be heard above the animal's fury?

The bear quickly figured out where Myles was and returned to the tree. Its roars were deafening, and it pushed against the tall pine, making it wave wildly. Then, to Myles's horror, the bear began to shinny its great bulk up the trunk. Even as Myles scrambled to move higher, one great paw slapped into his leg and pulled. He let out a shout, clinging to the trunk with all his strength. "God, help me!"

Shots rang out in rapid succession. Buck stood ten feet away in plain view, pumping bullets into the beast's back. The bear gave another roar, then a grunt, and dropped to the ground in a heap.

Myles hugged the tree trunk, laughing in hysteria. Relief made his arms go limp. Had he eaten breakfast, he would surely have lost it. Pain knifed through his leg. "Thank You, God. I'm alive."

"Amen." Buck's voice sounded equally shaky. "You all

right, Myles? I'm so sorry—I never dreamed my yell would bring the bear down on you like that. I thought he had you for a moment there."

"I think he got my leg. That beast went up a tree like a squirrel—I've never seen the like."

"It is a grizzly. I guessed it from the tracks, but I didn't believe my own eyes."

Myles tried to climb down the tree, feeling weaker than a kitten. His leg was wet. His head felt swimmy. "Check its neck, Buck. I have an idea he's wearing a collar, or used to be."

Buck bent over the carcass. "Biggest bear I've seen in years." He reached a hand into the coarse fur. "You guessed it, Myles. A leather collar with a short length of chain. Those rumors about the circus bear were true. I can't believe no one reported this!"

"No doubt the owner feared negative publicity. They probably expected to find the bear before they left, but he was too smart for them."

"Maybe he was smart, but a circus animal wouldn't know how to survive in the wild. Stealing stock was his only option. Look how skinny—no fat surplus for hibernation. He would never have lasted the winter. I can't help feeling a little sorry for the old bruin." Buck shoved the inert body with his boot.

"Not me. This isn't the first time that old buzzard came after me." Myles released his hold on a branch and dropped to the ground. His leg buckled. He fell to his knees and grabbed it. The hand came away red. "Buck, I need help."

Rushing to his side, Buck pulled out a knife and cut away the trousers. The smile lines around his eyes disappeared. "Looks nasty. Got to stop that bleeding."

twelve

Peace I leave with you, my peace I give unto you:
not as the world giveth, give I unto you.
Let not your heart be troubled, neither let it be afraid.
John 14:27

While Beulah mixed pancake batter, gazing dreamily through a frosty windowpane, she saw Jughead trot into the barnyard, riderless and wide-eyed. "Mama!" Dropping her work, she raced upstairs. "Mama, Jughead came home without Papa. Something bad has happened, I just know it!"

Violet nursed Daniel in the rocking chair. Her body became rigid; her blue eyes widened. "Let's not panic. Papa might have released Jughead for some reason." She bit her lip while Beulah wrung her hands. "Send Eunice over to tell Al. He'll know what to do."

Dead leaves whisked across the barnyard, dancing in a bitter wind. Frost lined the wilted flower border, and ice rimed the water troughs. His reins trailing, Jughead hunted for windfalls beneath the naked apple trees. Beulah's gentle greeting made the horse flinch and tremble. He allowed her to take his reins, however, and seemed grateful for her attentions. She patted his white shoulder, feeling cold sweat beneath his winter coat.

In the barn, Eunice was saddling Dolly. Excited and frightened, the younger girl chattered. "Can you believe how cold it is today? And yesterday I didn't even carry my coat to school. Good thing there's no school on Saturday or I wouldn't be home right now. Good thing Al hasn't left yet. Maybe he'll decide not to go to California after all. Maybe. . ."

Beulah tuned out her sister's prattle. If anything had happened to Papa or Myles. . .Beulah hauled Jughead's saddle from his back and hung it on the rack. Would Papa want her to blanket the horse now, or was Jughead warm enough with only his winter fur? Taking the gelding to his stall, she slipped off his bridle. The slimy snaffle bit rattled against his teeth, but Jughead was too good-natured to hold that against Beulah. He bumped her with his Roman nose and heaved a sigh, seeking reassurance.

Beulah patted his neck and rubbed his fuzzy brown ears, resting her cheek against his forelock. "Papa will be all right, Jughead. Don't worry."

"I'm leaving now, Beulah." Dolly's hooves clattered on the barn floor as Eunice mounted.

"Be careful. And hurry, Eunice."

After Dolly galloped up the driveway with Eunice clinging to her back, Beulah closed the barn door and returned to the house. Her face felt windburned when she removed her wraps.

Wandering from room to room, she looked for chores that needed doing. No one was hungry for pancakes, so she covered the batter. At last she decided to bake bread and cookies. The men might come home hungry. Her thoughts kept returning to Myles and Papa.

Dear God, please keep them safe! I love them both so much.

While the bread rose and the first batch of cookies baked, she sat at the table and tried to soak up the stove's radiated heat. Wind howled around the eaves and rattled the windows. Beulah shivered.

Violet entered the kitchen and sniffed. "It smells good in here, Beulah. You've been working hard." She spread a quilt on the floor and set Daniel on it, handing him a spoon and two bowls for playthings. Sitting at an awkward angle, he crowed and waved both hands in the air. He grinned at his mother, and Violet smiled back.

Beulah stared. "How can you be so calm, Mama? Papa could be in terrible danger out there, and it looks like snow again!" She waved a hand at the window.

"God is with him, Beulah. I've been praying since you told me about Jughead, and God assures me that He is in control. Remember Philippians 4:6–7: 'Be careful for nothing; but in every thing by prayer and supplication with thanksgiving let your requests be made known unto God. And the peace of God, which passeth all understanding, shall keep your hearts and minds through Christ Jesus.' If I chose to worry about Obie every time he went into a dangerous situation, I would be in a home for the insane by this time." Violet smiled.

Daniel leaned too far forward and fell on his face. Unfazed, he grabbed the spoon and batted it against a bowl.

Beulah studied her mother's expression. "But how, Mama? How can you trust God this way? You can't see Him, and you know that bad things happen sometimes."

Violet poured herself a cup of coffee. "When you truly know the Lord, you know that evil and pain are the farthest things from Him. He is all the joy and meaning in life, Dearest. Without Him, life is nothing. It's the Holy Spirit Who gives us peace, Beulah, along with love, kindness, and every other spiritual fruit. He doesn't force Himself into our lives—we have to allow Him to fill and use us for God's glory."

Beulah removed the cookies from the oven and put in another batch. "Last night I asked God to help me be kind to Marva, and He did. I have given my life to Jesus, and I know He is working in me, but I don't have the peace I see in your life and Papa's. Most of the time I don't even want to be kind and good. Hateful things come out of my mouth before I think them through!"

Violet rose and wrapped an arm around her daughter's drooping shoulders. "Darling, don't you understand that all people are that way? None of us in our own strength can be always kind or loving or unselfish. Those traits belong to God alone. And yet God can use anyone who is willing to be used by Him. You say He helped you last night? Then you know He can change your heart when you allow Him."

"I'm willing right now, but I might not be tomorrow,"

Beulah admitted. "You know how ornery I am."

Violet squeezed the girl's shoulders. "Yes, the tough part is surrendering your will to His will. I understand entirely. Where do you think you got your ornery nature? It wasn't from your father."

"Then how do you do it, Mama? How can you be so full of faith and patience and everything?"

"Remember when Jesus talked about taking up our cross daily? He meant that every day we must die to ourselves and let Him live through us. That is the only way to have lasting peace and joy in your life—and it's the only way to have faith through any crisis. When you know God well, you will understand how completely He can be trusted with your life."

Beulah nodded, thinking over her mother's words. She sampled a cookie, chewing slowly. "Mama, I need to talk with you about Myles. Last night, right before you told me to—"

Watchful began to bark from her post at the back window.

"Someone is coming," Violet said. Both women rushed to look outside. Behind them, Daniel began to cry. Violet hurried back to pick him up.

"They're back!" Beulah exclaimed. "Al and Eunice are with them."

"Thank the Lord!" Violet rejoined her at the window.

"I'm going out there to greet them," Beulah declared. She hurried to the entry hall for a coat and hat, then rushed down the steps and across the yard. "Papa! Myles, are you all right?" Both men looked pale and drawn.

Obie caught her before she could spook the horses. "We killed the bear, but not until after he took a swipe at Myles. Got to get the doctor out here right away. Help us take Myles into the house, and I'll ride to town."

"I'll go with you," Al offered. "I'm not leaving today. I'll catch a train next week. I can't run off to California when Myles is hurt."

Nobody argued. Beulah rushed back to the house to inform her mother, and together they decided Myles should have

Samuel's bed. The men carried Myles up the stairs just as Beulah tucked in the top bed sheet. The sight of his bloody boot and trouser leg stopped her breath for a long moment. "Oh, Myles!" she exclaimed. Her head began to feel light and foggy.

"It's not so bad. You should see the other guy." He gave her a crooked smile. "I'm pretty thirsty."

"I'll get you a drink. Do you want water or coffee or milk?"

"Water."

As she left the room, she heard her mother order quietly, "Al, help me cut the boot from his foot. Beulah, we need a basin of hot water."

"Yes, Mama." All the way downstairs and while she worked, Beulah prayed: *Lord, please fill me with your Spirit today and help me to show love, peace, joy, and every other fruit. Please help my dear Myles! Help the doctor to heal his leg like new. And please keep me from fainting when I see all that blood.*

She held the basin with towels to prevent sloshing water from burning her hands while she mounted the stairs. A bucket of cold water for Myles weighted her right arm.

"Put it there on the bureau," Violet said. "Thank you, Beulah. Al and Papa have gone for the doctor."

Beulah offered a dipper of well water to Myles. He propped himself on one elbow and drank. "Much better." When he returned the dipper, their hands touched. Beulah felt her lips tremble. She could not meet his gaze.

Beulah dropped the dipper into the bucket. On the floor at her feet lay the shredded shirt Obie had used to stanch Myles's blood. It was leaving a stain on the floorboards. Beulah closed her eyes and breathed deeply. *Don't think about it*, she told herself. She gingerly picked up the shirt and wrapped a clean sheet around it. Blood soaked through.

"You may toss out that old shirt." Violet was tearing a sheet into strips. "Then again, I suppose we can boil it and use it for rags."

Beulah trotted downstairs and put the bloody cloth in a pot

to boil, then ran outside and was sick behind the withered perennial bed. Her head still felt light afterward, but at least her stomach had settled. The cold, fresh air helped.

"The bleeding has slowed," Violet was saying when Beulah returned to the room, "but you'll have to be stitched."

"I thought as much." Myles looked pale.

"Beulah, will you please check on Daniel?" Violet asked. "I think I hear him stirring."

Beulah gave Myles a longing look, then hurried to obey her mother.

Daniel had pushed up with both hands to peer over the side of his cradle. His little face was crumpled into the pout that always appeared just before he started crying. He grinned when he saw Beulah and flopped back down on his face, crowing and kicking at his blankets. Beulah melted. "Oh, Sweetie, I do love you! I wish you would sleep right now, though."

"I'll take him for you, Beulah." Eunice stood in the doorway. Curls had escaped her braid to frame her round face, and the hem of her dress was soaked. Her blue eyes looked lost and lonely. "Is Myles going to die? You should have seen that bear. It was huge. Papa says it charged at Myles and he swung into a tree like a monkey." She wiped a fist across her eyes and sniffed. "Please let me take Daniel. I don't know what else to do." Tears clogged her voice.

A wave of love for her sister warmed Beulah's heart. "Myles lost a lot of blood, but I don't think he'll die. Of course you may take Daniel. You'd better change into dry clothes first. If you don't, you'll be coming down sick next thing, and we don't need that." Her voice softened. "Thank you for riding for help this morning. You're pretty wonderful."

Eunice's dimples appeared before her smile. She nodded and hurried to her room. Beulah settled into the rocking chair and cuddled Daniel close. He was too busy and awake to snuggle, so she let him sit up and amuse himself by playing with her buttons while she sang "Auld Lang Syne."

Eunice spread Daniel's blanket on the floor and set up his

blocks before she took the baby from Beulah. "We'll be fine. I think the doctor is here; someone arrived just now."

"Thank God! And Eunice, Al decided he's not leaving today." Beulah smiled at the overjoyed expression on her little sister's face. "He'll catch the train next week."

Eunice caught hold of Beulah's skirt as she whisked past. "Beulah, I'm sorry I said you were heartless. You love Myles, don't you?"

Biting her lip, Beulah nodded. "But don't you tell anyone!"

The dimples appeared again. "I won't. He's not Al, but I like him a lot."

Peace filled Beulah's heart as she returned to Samuel's bedroom. Next thing she knew, she was being shooed from the room. How she wished Myles would request her presence! Not that Mama would have allowed such a thing. Not that Beulah could have endured the sights or sounds of a sickroom without passing out on the floor.

Beulah hurried to the kitchen to prepare more coffee and cookies for everyone. Someone—Eunice?—had removed the batch of cookies from the oven and punched down the bread dough. It was ready to bake.

Dear God, it's hard to be helpful when all I want is to be with Myles. I guess this is the best way for me to serve today. Please help me to have a cheerful attitude and to give thanks.

Obie and Al were grateful for the hot food. Beulah joined their sober conversation midway through and gathered that someone besides Myles was hurt. "*Who* got shot last night, Papa? What happened?"

Obie wiped his nose with a handkerchief. "The sheriff. One of those drifters who's been causing trouble in town all month had a drop too much at the tavern last night and took offense when Boz offered him a night's rest in jail. Before anyone could react, the man pulled a gun and shot Boz from point-blank range."

Blood drained from Beulah's face. . .again. "Will he live, Papa?" she croaked.

Obie shook his head. "They carried him home, and Doc dug out the bullet, but he's afraid it nicked a lung. Boz has powder burns on his chest, and he has trouble breathing."

Beulah bit her lips and screwed up her face. The tears overflowed anyway.

Obie patted her hand. "Miss Amelia is taking care of him while Doc is here with Myles. Boz couldn't ask for better care. We just need to pray. He has peace about eternity, thank the Lord." Obie drew a shaky breath and blinked hard. "He's my oldest friend. The deputy is keeping order in town for the present. The man who shot Boz is behind bars. I'm hoping to visit him after church tomorrow."

"I'll go with you," Al offered.

"You could take him some of my cookies." Beulah wiped her face with her apron and tried to smile.

❦

Light snow fell Sunday, but Monday dawned clear and warmer. Eunice and Samuel threw snowballs back and forth as they left for school, but the snow blanket had dwindled to a few patches by noon.

While Mama nursed Daniel, Beulah peeked in to check on Myles. His foot lay propped on pillows. In repose, his pale face had a boyish look. His eyes opened, but Beulah slipped away before he spotted her. Violet had made it clear that Beulah was never to be alone with Myles in his sickroom.

Outside, Watchful began to bark. Beulah went to her own room and peered down at the driveway. "Mama, someone is coming. I don't recognize the horses."

Violet sounded harassed. "Would you greet our guest and make excuses for me, Dear? I'll be down when Daniel is finished."

Beulah untied her apron and hung it on a hook, patted her hair, and opened the door. An elderly woman stood on the top step. Behind her, the buggy turned around and disappeared up the driveway. "Hello, Dear. Is this Obadiah Watson's home?"

"Yes, it is."

Watchful suddenly rushed past the woman into the house, whisked Beulah's skirts, and bounded up the stairs. "I'm so sorry," Beulah gasped. "That was my brother's dog."

The lady straightened her bonnet. "Does a man named Myles Trent work here?"

"Yes, but he does not live here."

The lady's face fell. "But they told me. . .Oh, dear, and I let that hired rig go. . .I was so sure Myles would be here."

Beulah hurried to explain, "No, don't worry—you see, he is here right now. Upstairs in bed. He was injured the other day. Are you—Could you be his grandmother?"

The woman lifted a trembling hand to her lips. "Yes, I am Virginia Van Huysen. Is my grandson expected to live?"

Her tragic eyes startled Beulah. "Oh, yes!" she quickly assured. "He is recovering nicely. It was a bear that attacked him."

"I see." The woman looked bewildered. "My Myles was attacked by a bear?"

Beulah recalled her manners. "Please come inside. My mother will be down in a few minutes; she is caring for my baby brother. I'm sure Myles will wish to see you."

Mrs. Van Huysen gave her a weak smile and stepped inside. "I hope so. I'm sorry, Child—it has been a long and tedious journey. My train arrived in town only this morning. Mr. Poole was supposed to meet me in Chicago, but he did not appear."

"I see." Beulah said nothing. She could neither ask questions nor remain silent. The lady seated herself on the horsehair davenport at Beulah's invitation. They sat and stared at one another.

"Would you like me to tell Myles that you have arrived?"

"He did not know I was coming." There was sadness in the woman's reply. "How old are you, Child?"

"Eighteen. I am Beulah Fairfield. Obadiah Watson is my stepfather. Myles has worked for him these past three years, mostly during the summers."

"I am pleased to make your acquaintance, Miss Fairfield.

You are a pretty child. Do you play the piano?" She indicated Violet's instrument.

"A little. Nothing to compare with Myles. He played for us the other night for the first time. It was amazing."

Mrs. Van Huysen lifted her brows. "So, he still can play. Hmm. Did he sing for you?"

Beulah could not help but smile. "Yes! It was wonderful. He told us that he was a concert pianist in New York, and he told us his real name for the first time. Did you receive his letter?"

"Letter? Myles has not written to me in years."

"But he did! Just last week. He wanted to apologize to you for running away to join the circus when he was a boy. Did Myles live with you always?"

"The boys lived with me after their parents died."

"I didn't know his parents were dead. My father died years ago, but my mother is happy with Mr. Watson. He is a good father to us." Beulah paused. "Did you say 'the boys'? Does Myles have a brother?"

Mrs. Van Huysen suddenly rose. "Please take me to Myles now. I can wait no longer."

Beulah led her to the staircase. "This way, please."

Mrs. Van Huysen worked her way up the stairs. Beulah wanted to offer her arm for support but feared rejection. "This way," she repeated, pushing open the door to Samuel's bedroom.

Myles appeared to be asleep. Blankets covered him to the chin, and his eyes were closed. "Myles?" Beulah whispered, moving to the far side of the bed. He did not stir. The room still smelled of blood, ether, and pain.

Mrs. Van Huysen stood at his other side. "Myles, my dear boy!" Her lips moved, but no other sound emerged. Tears trickled over her withered cheeks.

Beulah touched Myles's shoulder. "Myles, wake up. There is someone here to see you." Her own eyes burned. "Myles!" She gripped his shoulder and shook gently. Her fingers touched warm bare skin. Startled, she jerked her hand away.

His eyes popped open and focused on her face. "Beulah. I was dreaming about you." His hazy smile curled her toes. His hand lifted toward her face.

"Look who is here to see you, Myles," she whispered, unable to speak loudly. She glanced at his grandmother, and a tear slipped down her cheek.

Myles turned his head. Beulah saw his eyes go wide, and his mouth fell open. A moment later he was sitting up, clutching Mrs. Van Huysen and nearly pulling the lady from her feet. "Gram!" His voice was a ragged sob.

Beulah crept from the room.

thirteen

Thou wilt keep him in perfect peace,
whose mind is stayed on thee:
because he trusteth in thee.
Isaiah 26:3

"You're so tiny, Gram. Did you shrink, or have I grown?" Myles asked.

Virginia patted his hand and smoothed his forehead, just as she had during his childhood illnesses. She smiled, but her expression was far away. "You must tell me about Monte sometime, Myles. Right now is convenient for me."

He pulled his hand out of her grasp and ran it over his rumpled hair. "I know. I've been hiding things too long, from myself. . .from everyone." He drew a deep breath and released it in a sigh, praying silently for strength. "This won't be easy."

Virginia watched him with sad yet peaceful eyes.

"Monte was wild, Gram. I know you thought he was a good boy, but it was all a sham. He loved to gamble, drink, and smoke. . .although I can say with confidence that he was never a womanizer. You raised us to respect women, and Monte kept that shred of decency as far as I know. With his charm, he might have been worse than he was."

Tears pooled in his grandmother's eyes, but she nodded. "I knew, Myles. It nearly broke my heart to see the way you two boys fought and despised each other. I prayed for wisdom and did everything I could to encourage love and respect between you. It never happened. For some reason, Monte considered you a rival from the day you were born."

Myles sat stunned. "You knew? I thought you doted on him."

"Certainly. I doted on the both of you. What grandmother

doesn't dote on her grandsons, flawed though they may be?"

"Then why did you keep me isolated from everyone except private tutors and force me to practice for hours every day? It was a terrible life for a boy! I thought you hated me and loved Monte."

Virginia looked stunned. "I wanted the best for you, Myles. God gave you a wondrous gift, and I felt it my duty to give you every opportunity to develop and enjoy that gift of music. I thought your complaints stemmed from laziness, and I refused to listen. Oh, my dear, how wrong I was! My poor boys!" Wiping her eyes, she insisted, "Tell me about Monte. I must know."

"When you sent him after me, he took advantage of the opportunity to sample every pleasure the world had to offer. He was delighted to escape his responsibilities. He did plan to return someday, but then circumstances prevented it."

Virginia shook her head. "I knew I had lost him. Releasing him to find you was a last effort to show him that I trusted and respected him as a man. He proved himself unworthy, as I feared. He did write to me occasionally over the years, however, as you did. I never understood why that precious correspondence ended."

Myles absently unbuttoned his undervest. "The last place we were together was Texas; you knew that much. We had a steady job brush-popping longhorns for a big rancher. Monte started running with a group of gamblers. They were the ruin of him. It wasn't long before he started rustling a beef here and there to support his habit, and the boss became suspicious."

Tears trickled down Virginia's cheeks again, but she nodded for him to continue.

Myles twined a loose string around his finger and tugged. "Then all of a sudden Monte changed. I don't know exactly what happened—well, maybe I do—but anyway, one day he was wild, angry, and miserable; the next day he was peaceful, calm, and had this radiant joy about him. He told me that he had made his life right with God. I thought he had lost his mind. Both of us hated church and anything to do with religion, yet here was Monte saying he had found Jesus Christ. He tried to talk with me about God—even gave me a Bible for my birthday."

"Thank You, Jesus!" Virginia moaned into her handkerchief.

"One day we were riding herd, almost ready to start a drive north. Monte was across from me, hunting strays in the arroyos. A group of riders approached him. I took my horse up on a small bluff and watched. I had a bad feeling—something about the situation made me nervous. The best I can figure, the riders were men to whom Monte owed money, probably demanding payment. I saw Monte's horse rear up; Monte fell off backward and vanished. The sound of a shot reached me an instant later. Panic spread through the herd. Within seconds I was riding for my life, hemmed in on every side by fear-crazed longhorns."

The string broke free and his button dropped beneath the blankets.

"And Monte?"

"I never found him, Gram. By the time we got that herd straightened out—a good bit smaller than it was when the stampede started—we were miles from the location of the fight, and it was pouring rain. I hunted for days, but found no trace of Monte or his mustang. The horse never returned to the remuda; it must have died in the stampede, too."

Virginia sobbed quietly.

"I don't know if the men who killed Monte were aware that I witnessed his murder, but I didn't take chances. I was nineteen, scared, stricken with regret and sorrow. I hightailed it out of Texas and never went back. Once or twice I thought about writing to you, but shame prevented it. Not until God straightened me out this summer did I have the courage to confess my role in Monte's death."

"You weren't to blame, Myles." The idea roused Virginia from her grief.

He sniffed ruefully. "Had I not run away from home, Monte would never have been in Texas."

"Then he most likely would have died in a back alley in Manhattan. It is not given us to know what might have been, my boy. We can only surrender what actually is to the Lord and trust Him to work His perfect will in our lives." Virginia's voice gained strength as she spoke. "Monte is safe with the Lord, for which fact I am eternally grateful. Myles, Dear, can you ever forgive me for my failings as a grandmother?"

Myles nodded. A muscle in his cheek twitched. "I forgive you, Gram. You meant well." He blinked, feeling as if a small chunk had broken from the burden he carried. To his surprise, forgiving his grandmother was an agreeable experience. Love welled up in his heart, and he opened his arms to her.

Weeping and smiling, Virginia fell into his embrace without apparent regard for her dignity.

❦

Beulah carried a tray upstairs and knocked at the closed door. The voices inside stopped, and Mrs. Van Huysen opened the door. "That looks lovely, Dear. Thank you." She stepped aside, and Beulah carried the tray to the bureau.

"Are you two having a good visit? Were you comfortable last night, Mrs. Van Huysen?"

"Yes, Dear. Thank you for the use of your bedroom. I'm sorry to put everyone to such inconvenience."

"It is no trouble. We are all pleased to meet Myles's grandmother."

More than a day had passed since Virginia's arrival. Beulah's family had begun to wonder if the two Van Huysens would ever rejoin the world.

Myles eyed the steaming bowls and the stack of fresh bread slices. "What kind of stew?"

Beulah felt her face grow warm. She gave his grandmother an uncertain glance. "Bear."

Virginia's face showed mild alarm.

Myles laughed aloud. "Poetic justice. I hope he was a tender bear. Don't worry, Gram; Beulah is the best cook in the state, with the possible exception of her mother."

"I don't doubt it."

"I hope it's good stew," Beulah said weakly. "Papa says the bear was skinny and tough. He showed me how to prepare it so it would taste better, but I don't know if you'll like it."

Myles shoved himself upright. "Beulah, will you ask Al to feed Pushy? She must be wondering what happened to me."

Beulah avoided looking at him. "Al says Pushy is lonely but well. She reminded him to feed her. No kittens yet."

"You need to take a look at the stitches in my leg, Beulah. There are fifty-seven. Doc did a great job of patchwork. Maybe you could learn a few new designs for your next quilt. Beulah sews beautiful quilts, Gram. She can make almost anything."

"Indeed?"

"Did you see the bear when they brought it in, Beulah? Wasn't he immense? You should have seen that monster climb a tree. He would have had me for sure if Buck hadn't packed him with lead. Say, that water looks good. Would you pour me a drink?"

Beulah felt his gaze as she poured two glasses of water from the pitcher. She glanced at his grandmother and caught an amused smile on the lady's face.

Virginia suddenly rose from her chair and smacked Myles's hand. "Stop that belly rubbing. Never could break you of that." She addressed Beulah obliquely. "Myles suffered chronic stomachaches as a child. He used to wake me every night, crying for his mother. At least he no longer totes around a blanket."

Myles slumped back against the pillows. "No secret is sacred."

Beulah smiled. He would be embarrassed for certain if she gave her opinion of his habit—she found it endearing.

"Myles was a sickly, scrawny child—all eyes and nose. It's amazing what time can do for a man. I never would have known you in a crowd, Myles—although one look into your eyes would have told me. Doesn't he have beautiful eyes, Beulah? They are like his mother's eyes, changing hue to suit his emotions. I would call them hazel."

"Sometimes they look gold like a cat's," Beulah observed.

"Has he told you that he was being groomed for opera? His beautiful voice, his ability to play almost any piece the audience might request, and his subtle humor packed in the crowds. He was truly a marvel—so young, yet confident and composed. Even as a little child, he was mature beyond his years. I thought I was doing the best thing for him, helping him reach the peak of his ability. How wrong a grandmother can be!" She shook her head sadly.

"We've already discussed this, Gram. It's in the past and forgiven, remember?" Myles sounded embarrassed.

"Myles told me about the letter he wrote last week." Virginia shook her head. "I never received it. My private detective, Mr. Poole, recently discovered Myles's whereabouts after long years of searching. I find it odd that Myles wrote to me even as I was coming to see him. But the Lord does work in mysterious ways."

"God told me to write to you, Gram," Myles said gruffly, "even though He knew you were coming."

"At any rate, I plan to telegraph Myles's old agent tomorrow and set up a return performance. The musical world will be agog; his disappearance made the papers for months. His reappearance will take the world by storm, I am certain."

"Gram," Myles began, sounding somewhat irritated.

Beulah backed toward the door. "That's wonderful. You had better eat before the stew gets cold. I'll be back for the dishes."

She heard Myles call her name as she ran down the steps, but she could not return and let them see her distress. *Myles is leaving!*

❦

"Beulah is a pretty thing and well-spoken," Virginia commented. "Exquisite figure, although I'm sure you have noticed that fact."

"I have."

"Your fancy for the child is evident, and even I can see why she attracts you." Her gaze shifted to Myles, and she pursed her lips. "The bluest blood in New York runs in Van Huysen veins."

"Blended with the good red blood of soap merchants, sea captains, and a black sheep or two. From all I hear, some of Beulah's ancestors might have looked down their aristocratic noses at one or two of my wild and woolly ancestors." His mustache curled into a smirk.

Virginia merely poked at her stew.

"So you like Beulah, Gram?" Myles dipped a chunk of bread into his stew and took a large bite.

"I suspect there is more to that inquiry than idle curiosity. Do you intend to wed the child?"

"I do." One cheek bulged as he spoke.

His grandmother considered this information. "Would she blend into our society, Myles? Her manners are charming, but they are country manners, nonetheless."

"If she won't blend in, then I wouldn't either. It's been a long time since I lived in your world." Myles ate with relish.

Virginia frowned. "Yours is a veneer of wilderness, I'm certain. Cultured habits will return, given the proper surroundings. I do hope you plan to shave soon. Facial hair does not become you."

"It was a disguise. Not a good one, but it fooled me." Myles smiled wryly. "All of this is immaterial, since, as you know, I do not intend to remain in New York. One farewell concert, sell the business, and back here I come to purchase a farm." His voice quivered with excitement.

Virginia lifted a trembling hand to her lips. "Um, Myles. . ."

"Buck Watson told me again and again that God blesses when we surrender our lives, and I'm living proof of that fact. It struck me one day that my resistance to facing my past was preventing me from having the future I longed for. You can stay in Long Island if you like, Gram, or we could sell that old house and move you out here. There's room in the Thwaite farmhouse, and I plan to build on anyway. The farm needs money and work, that's certain, but neither should be a problem."

Virginia finally succeeded in breaking into his soliloquy. "About the business. . .there is something you need to know, Myles."

❦

Beulah scooped the mess of raw egg and shattered shells from the hardwood floor and dumped it into a pail. Goo had settled in the cracks between boards.

"I didn't mean to, Beulah. The floor was slippery, and I fell flat." Samuel hovered around her, shaking his hands in distress. "Mama needed those eggs. I feel awful."

Beulah sat back on her heels and sighed. "The chickens will lay more eggs tomorrow, I'm sure. We still have two from yesterday. Don't worry about it. I'm thankful you're not hurt."

Samuel crouched beside her. "Are you feeling all right, Beulah? Is Myles dying? Is Sheriff Boz dying? Why are you being so nice?"

Beulah frowned, then chuckled. "As far as I know, no one is dying. Papa says the sheriff is holding his own. I simply don't see any point in being angry about smashed eggs. You didn't intend to break them, and someone has to clean it up. I'm not busy right now like Mama is, so I'm right for the job."

Her brother laid a hand on her shoulder. "Thanks, Beulah. You're a peach." With a fond pat, he hurried from the room.

When the floor was no longer sticky, Beulah sat back with a satisfied sigh. "That wasn't so bad."

"Beulah," Samuel called from another room. "Mama wants you to collect the dishes from Myles's room. And can you set beans to soak?"

"I will." When the beans were covered and soaking, Beulah washed her hands and checked her reflection in the blurry mirror. Her hair was reasonably neat, and the chapping around her mouth had cleared. She touched her lower lip, recalling Myles's ardent kisses. "Will he ever kiss me again?" she whispered.

Glancing at the ceiling, she sighed again. *Lord, please give me peace about the future. I know You are in control, but I always want to know about things right now! Please help me to control my emotions around Myles and to seek Your will.*

Minutes later, Beulah knocked at the bedroom door. "Myles?"

Silence.

She pushed open the door. He lay with arms folded across his chest, staring out the window. "Myles, do you mind if I collect your dishes?"

He did not so much as bat an eye. Biting her lower lip, Beulah began to load the dinner dishes onto her tray. Mrs. Van Huysen had picked at her food. Myles must have enjoyed his stew.

"Please stay," Myles begged as Beulah prepared to lift the tray. He reached out a hand. She was startled to see that his eyelids were red and swollen.

"Myles, what's wrong? Where is your grandmother?" She wrapped his cold hand within both of hers. "Are you hurting?"

His other hand fiddled with a buttonhole on his undervest; the corresponding button was missing. "Yes." He pressed her hand to his cheek and heaved a shaky sigh.

"I'm so sorry!" Beulah settled into the chair beside his bed. "Would you like me to read to you?"

"No. Don't go so far away."

Beulah blinked. "Far? I'm right next to you. Where is Mrs. Van Huysen?"

"Lying down, I think. I don't care. Nothing matters anymore."

She reached out to feel his forehead. "You're cool and damp. Would you like another blanket?"

When she would have returned to the chair, he grabbed her around the waist and pulled until her feet left the floor. Sprawled across him, Beulah felt his face press into her neck. "Myles, let me go! What if my mother walked in right now? She would murder me!"

"I need you, Beulah. Just hold me, please! I won't do anything indecent, I promise."

Hearing tears in his voice, she stilled. "Myles, what is

wrong?" Her hand came to rest on his upper arm. It was hard as stone. His entire body was as tense as a bowstring.

"Do you love me, Beulah?"

Her teeth began to chatter from pure nerves. Something was not right. She felt a terrible heaviness in her spirit. "Yes, I love you. I do. Myles, whatever is wrong? I'm frightened." Pushing up with one arm, she regarded his face. "You were bright and cheerful when I brought lunch. Is the pain that bad? I'll get Mama."

"No!" He gripped her wrist. His eyes were glassy and intense. "Will you marry me right away? We can start over somewhere else, maybe homestead a place."

She shook her head in confusion. "I thought you planned to buy the Thwaite farm and settle here. Why should we marry right away? You're acting so strange, Myles."

He emitted a bark of laughter. "Plans? I have no more plans. Not ever. Plans involve depending on someone else. I will never again trust anyone but myself. And you, of course. You'll be my wife. We can live by ourselves out West."

The dread in Beulah's chest increased. "Please tell me what has happened." She twisted her arm, trying to escape his vise-like grip.

He suddenly released her and flung both forearms over his face. "Same old story. I trust someone, they let me down. Everyone I have ever depended on has failed me. Everyone. Most of all God. As soon as I start trusting Him even the slightest bit, the world caves in. If you desert me, too, Beulah, I think I'll crawl away and die."

She reached a hand toward his arched chest, then drew it back. "But God will never fail you. Why do you think He let you down?"

Myles sat up in a rush of flying blankets. Eyes that reminded Beulah of a cornered cougar's blazed into her soul, and an oath blasted from Myles's lips. His white teeth were bared. "Enough of this insanity! The entire concept of a loving, all-powerful God is absurd. A fairy tale we've been force-feeding children for generations. A superstition from the Dark Ages. I don't ever want to hear you talk about God to me again, do you hear?"

Beulah's mouth dropped open.

His fury faded. "Don't look at me like I'm some kind of monster! I need you, Beulah!" Flinging the blankets aside, Myles swung his legs over the far side of the bed and tried to stand on his good leg.

Seeing him sway, she sprang around the foot of the bed. "What are you doing? Myles, get back in bed or I'll call Papa." She stopped cold, realizing that he wore nothing but winter underwear. Hot blood flooded her face, and she rushed back to stand by the door.

He whipped a blanket from the bed and wrapped it around his waist. Jaw set, he hopped to the window and looked down on bare trees and blowing snow. "That's how I feel inside: cold, gray, and lifeless."

"That's because you've turned your back on God." Beulah was surprised to hear herself speak. "What happened to you, Myles? Why are you acting this way?"

He huffed. "I'll tell you what happened. For years Buck has been telling me about God, about salvation. Finally I decided to try this thing out, trusting God. I wrote to Gram. I started giving God credit for the good things happening in my life. I even started believing that He was with me. When I read the Bible it was as if He talked to me."

Beulah studied his broad shoulders and felt her dreams crumbling.

"I began to believe that He had wonderful plans for my life—marriage with you, the farm I've always wanted, and friends who like me for myself, not because I'm a Van Huysen. I've never wanted the money; I've been proud to support myself and lean on no one. . .except maybe Buck. But since God told me to reconcile with Gram, I figured He must intend me to make use of my inheritance. I didn't want much; just enough to buy a farm and set us up with a good living. Then I found out that you loved me—life was looking incredibly

;ood. Gram came, asked me to forgive her, and I did. Great tuff. Everything coming together."

He fell silent.

Beulah settled into a chair, hands clenched in her lap.

"Then the cannonball drops: There is no money. The family riend who ran the Van Huysen Soap Company mismanaged t into bankruptcy, sold out to another manufacturer, and is ow president of that company. He swindled it all away and eft Gram holding massive debts. She sold off most of our tock and commercial properties to pay the debts, then mortgaged the family house to pay for the detectives who found ne. There is no money. None."

Beulah tried to sound sympathetic. "Don't the police know ow that man cheated your grandmother? Isn't there something you could do to help her?"

"There is no money to pay for lawyers, and apparently Mr. Roarke covered his legal tracks. It looks as shady as the botom of a well, but no one can prove anything."

"Poor Mrs. Van Huysen. I can understand why you are ipset. Had you been there to keep an eye on the business, this night not have happened to her."

Myles turned to fix her with a glare. "Don't you undertand, Beulah? Gram is fine; she still has the old house and a mall stipend to live on. The money lost was *my* money! This s the end of *my* dream. I have no money to buy a farm, and I an't support a family on my pay as a hired hand. We cannot tay here. Either I must return to New York and try to break ack into the music world—which would not be an easy task io matter what Gram says—or I must head out West and find and to homestead."

Beulah's chest heaved, and her heart thudded against her ibs. That heavy, ugly feeling weighed on her spirit. "So vhen it looks like God is answering your prayers the way 'ou want, you believe in Him. As soon as things don't go 'our way, you decide He doesn't exist? That isn't faith, Ayles. That is opportunism. And I thought *I* was a selfish person! I don't care what you decide to do. Whatever it is you'll do it without me."

Picking up the tray, she stalked from the room.

fourteen

And Jesus answered and said unto him,
What wilt thou that I should do unto thee?
Mark 10:51a

l entered the sickroom without knocking. "Myles, you
on't believe what happened!" Spotting Mrs. Van Huysen, he
illed off his hat. "Hello, Ma'am."

"Good morning, Albert," Virginia responded cordially.

"I sure enjoyed visiting with you last night. Myles, do you
now this grandmother of yours whupped me at checkers? It
as an outright slaughter."

"Myles never cared for the game," Virginia said when
[yles remained silent. "He is good at chess, however." A
oment later, she rose and gathered her embroidery. "I'll let
ou boys chat awhile." The door clicked shut behind her.

Al settled into the empty chair, long legs splayed. "It stinks
here. Like medicine."

Myles tried to scratch his leg beneath the bandage. The skin
owing around the white cloth was mottled green and pur-
e. "What's the news from town? Doc tells me it looks like
oz will pull through."

"If good nursing has anything to do with it, Boz will be
ick on his feet within the week. From all I hear, Miss Amelia
eats him like a king." Al's eyes twinkled. "She had him
oved to her boardinghouse, and her front parlor is now a
ospital room. Nothing more interesting to a woman than a
ounded man, but I guess you know all about that."

Myles grunted. "So what's your big news?"

Al slipped a letter from his chest pocket. "Today I got this
tter from my folks asking me not to come west until spring.

Can you believe it? Today! Think about it: If you hadn’t let tha bear rip your leg off, I would have been on my way by no and missed their letter. No wonder I didn’t have peace abou leaving! They don’t even want me yet. I have no idea what I’ do with my farm next year, but it doesn’t matter—God wi provide, and I’ve got all winter to think and prepare. So if yo need to go to New York, don’t hesitate on my account.”

Myles tried to smile. “That’s good news, Al. I felt guilt about delaying your trip.”

“Now that you’re rich and all, you won’t be needing a far job, I reckon,” Al said, looking regretful. “I feel funny abou things I must have said to you in the last year or two, m thinking you had less education and fewer advantages than had!” His grin was crooked. “That will teach me to judg people by appearance.”

“You always treated me well, Al. You have nothing fo which to apologize.”

“Why are you so gloomy? Is your leg hurting?”

The innocent question sparked Myles’s wrath. He bit bac a sharp reply and folded his arms on his chest, staring out th window.

“Hmm. Beulah is moody, too. My powers of deduction te me that all is not well in paradise.”

“Shove off, Al. I’m not in the mood for your jokes.” Myle scowled.

Al pursed his lips in thought. “Want to talk with Buck?”

“I want to get out of this house, pack up, and head fo Montana.”

“What happened, Myles? I thought your life was goin great. Beulah loves you, you’ve cleared things up with you grandmother, you’ve got a music career and money to burn.”

“I’m not rich, Al. The money’s gone.”

“Oh. All the money?”

“Every cent.”

Al looked confused. “But Beulah wouldn’t care whethe you’re rich or not. She loved you as a hired hand.”

"Whatever I do, wherever I go, she says she's not going with me. Guess she only loved me if I stayed here in town." Bitterness left a foul taste in his mouth.

"That doesn't sound like Beulah. She could make a home anywhere if she set her mind to it, and she's crazy about you, Myles."

Myles gave a mirthless sniff.

"Sure you don't want to talk to Buck?"

"I know what he'll say. He will tell me I need to forgive those who have wronged me and give control of my life over to God. I've heard it all before."

Al lifted a brow. "Sooo, tell me what's wrong with that answer? Sounds to me as if the truth pricks your pride, Pal."

Myles rolled his eyes.

"C'mon, Myles. Think this through. Are you content and filled with joy right now?"

Myles slashed a glare at Al, but his friend never blinked. "Fine. Don't answer that. Think about this: How could your life be worse if God were in control of it?"

Myles opened his mouth, then closed it. His head fell back against the headboard. "I've never had control anyway."

"Exactly. You're at the mercy of circumstances with no one to turn to. The only things you can truly control in your life are your behavior and your reactions."

"Sometimes I can't even control myself."

"Without God, we're all losers. Look at Buck. The stuff that happened to him was like your worst nightmare. He could be the most bitter, angry person you ever met, but he chose to trust God with his life, and look at him now!"

Myles nodded. "And you, too. You didn't get angry about Beulah."

Al shrugged. "It wouldn't have done any good to get mad. Anyone can see she isn't in love with me, and to be honest, my heart isn't broken. The point is, once you decide to trust God with things, He turns your messed-up life into something great. I'm not saying you'd have it easy from then on, or that all your dreams would come true; but no matter what hap-pens, your life would be a success. The Bible says in Firs Peter, 'Humble yourselves therefore under the mighty hand o God, that he may exalt you in due time.' You can never lif yourself up no matter how hard you try."

After a moment's thought, Myles lowered his chin an shook his head. "I don't see it, Al. I understand that God is fa above me, holy and just, almighty and righteous, but loving? don't know God that way. Sure, He saved me from the bea but look what has happened to me since."

"When was the last time you read about Jesus?"

"The last time I read the Bible? I was reading in Genesi the other night."

"I think you need to read the Gospels now. The Ol Testament is important, too, but you need to understand abou Jesus first. Where is your Bible?"

"At our house next to my bed. Don't bring it here, Al. want to go home. Can you talk Buck into taking me home It's driving me crazy, being here in the same house wit Beulah. She hasn't spoken to me since we fought yesterday Gram is good to me, but I'm getting cabin fever."

Al looked into his eyes and gave a short nod. "I'll talk t Buck."

❦

Beulah watched the wagon disappear up the drive. Her eye were dry. Her heart felt as leaden as the sky. Returning to he seat, she picked up her piecework and took a disintereste stitch.

Violet observed her from across the parlor. "The hous already seems quiet, doesn't it? I will miss having Virgini around to chat with. She is the most interesting lady. Sh refused my offer to stay here. I hope she will be comfortabl at the men's house. They don't have an indoor pump, yo know, and the furnishings are rather crude."

"Is Daniel sleeping?" Beulah asked in her most casual tone

"Yes. Samuel is at Scott's house, and Eunice is reading. Di

'ou hear Al's news?" Violet snipped a thread with her teeth.

"Several times over. I told Eunice first; then she told *me* ̣bout three times so far. I'm glad he's not leaving for awhile. Ve would all miss him. I think Eunice has romantic feelings or Al."

Violet chuckled. "I've noticed. She has good taste. Maybe 'll have Albert for a son-in-law someday after all. I hope so. Ie's a dear boy."

Beulah concentrated on tying a knot. "She's only thirteen, Aama. Maybe I should have married him."

Violet's hands dropped to her lap. "Pardon?"

Beulah winced, wishing she had kept the stray thought to ierself. "Al wouldn't marry me now if I proposed to him nyself, and I'm not in love with him anyway, but I can't ielp wondering if I couldn't have been happily married to im. After all, lots of people make marriages of convenience nd end up happy together. Al is annoying, but he's steady nd safe."

Violet lowered her chin and stared at her daughter. "What bout Myles?"

Beulah pressed her lips together and jerked at a tangle in er thread. "Myles is not the man I thought he was. He is selfsh and bitter." She swallowed hard.

Setting aside her mending, Violet joined her daughter on ie couch. "Tell me."

Beulah leaned against Violet. Her shoulders began to shake. Viping her eyes, she grumbled, "I hate crying, Mama, but it eems as if every time I try to talk about something important, start bawling."

"It's a woman's lot in life, Darling." Violet pushed a lock of oose hair behind her daughter's ear and smiled. "I understand, believe me."

Between sobs and sniffles, Beulah poured out her heartache nd disappointment. ". . .so I told him he could go without ie. I thought he was kind and wise, Mama, but yesterday he cted like a brute. And all because of some money he doesn't

have. I'm so thankful I found out what he is really like befor
I married him!"

Violet stared at the fireplace, pondering her reply. "So nov
Myles is a brute. All the good things you loved about hir
mean nothing."

Beulah wiped her eyes and nose with a handkerchief. "I coul
never be happily married to a man with such a terrible tempe
Mama. He swore in my presence and never apologized!"

"If Myles has truly turned his back on the Lord, then
agree that you should not marry him. But if, as your pap
believes, he is on the verge of surrender, it would be a sham
for you to give up on him. He adores you, Beulah, and I thin
he would make you an excellent husband."

Beulah's head popped up. "Mama! How can you say th
after what I just told you? He told me never to mention God'
name in his presence again!"

"He was distraught. I'm sure he didn't mean it. I unde
stand he had a long talk with Al about God this afternoo
and he plans to start reading the New Testament when h
gets home today. Darling, every man has faults. I hope yo
realize that. Even Al would lose his temper, given the rigl
provocation."

"Papa never shouts at you."

A dimple appeared near Violet's mouth. "No, but that'
because he talks softly when he gets angry. The angrier he i
the softer his voice."

"You don't mean it, Mama," Beulah said, eyes wide.

Violet rubbed a little circle on the girl's back. "I mea
every word. Darling, you had better learn quickly that onl
God can offer you complete security and contentment. N
man can fulfill your every need, and most of them wouldn
want to try. The average man enters marriage thinking that
wife's purpose is to fulfill *his* needs. Unless you recognize th
fact that all people are basically selfish, you will be in for
rude awakening when you marry. Myles has plenty of fault
but so have you, my dear."

"If people are so terribly selfish, how can a marriage ever be happy?"

"That's where the Lord makes a difference. In His strength, you and I can learn to love our men with all their human flaws and failings. That is one of the greatest joys of marriage: to give and give of yourself to please your beloved. Usually a good man will respond in kind, but you must understand that there is never a guarantee of this. Your part is to love at all times, without reservation."

Beulah wilted. "How can I do that, Mama? You know how selfish I am!"

"In the Lord's strength, Dear. If you truly love Myles, you will accept him just as he is and be grateful for the opportunity to shower him with the love and attention he craves from you. There are few things in life more fulfilling than pleasing your husband, Beulah." Violet spoke with the authority of experience.

Beulah sat straighter. "I want to be exactly like you, Mama. You make Papa so happy that he glows when you're near. I want to make Myles that happy."

Violet squeezed her shoulders. "That's my girl! Now you keep on praying for Myles, and when he is ready to receive your love, I think you will know it."

Beulah hugged her mother. "You're wonderful. I feel so much better! Now, I have this idea for my wedding dress that I've been wanting to discuss with you. Do you have a moment?"

Eyes twinkling, Violet nodded.

❦

Pushy kneaded a dent for herself in the middle of Myles's back. He groaned when she settled down. "You must weigh a ton, Cat. When are you going to fire off those kittens?"

Pushy purred, vibrating against him. "You really missed me, didn't you?" Her affectionate greeting had warmed his heart.

He returned to his reading. The book was fascinating. For

the first time in his life, Myles could visualize Jesus among the people, teaching, healing, loving.

The parable of the unforgiving servant in Matthew, chapter eighteen, struck a nerve. He recognized himself in the cruel, vindictive man who punished a debtor after he himself had been forgiven a much larger debt. The simple story was an eloquent reprimand and admonition.

"I understand, Jesus," Myles said, bowing his head. "This story is about me. Please forgive me for my anger at Monte. I want to forgive him as You forgave me. If he's there with You now, please tell him for me. Tell him I love him. I forgive Mama for dying and leaving me behind. She must have been terribly lonely after Father was killed in the war. And I forgive Mr. Roarke for swindling us, too. I don't imagine he's deriving much true pleasure from his ill-gotten gains. I feel almost sorry for him. You know that the real reason I refused to forgive people all those years was pride. I thought I was better than others. I was wrong."

Humility was an easy burden in comparison to the bitter load he had carried for so many years. Myles felt free and relaxed, yet still rather empty.

"Where is the joy, God? Are You really here with me? What's wrong with me? Maybe I'm spiritually blind."

Pushy purred on.

Sighing, Myles returned to the Book. The story enthralled him, and when he reached the end of Matthew, he continued on into Mark, absorbed in the story of Jesus from a slightly different perspective. His eyes were growing heavy when he reached chapter ten, the story of blind Bartimaeus begging at the roadside.

Then, for some reason, he was wide-awake. His mind pictured the pitiful man in rags who cried out, "Jesus, Son of David, have mercy on me!"

Jesus stopped and asked the fellow what he wanted. Jesus didn't overlook the poor and helpless among His people. He cared about the blind man.

Myles read the next part aloud. " 'The blind man said unto him, Lord, that I might receive my sight.

" 'And Jesus said unto him, Go thy way; thy faith hath made thee whole. And immediately he received his sight, and followed Jesus in the way.' "

Myles stopped and read it again. Slowly his eyes closed and his hands formed into fists. The cry echoed from his own heart. "Lord, I want to see! Please, help me to see You as You truly are."

He contemplated Jesus. "The kindest man who has ever lived. He came to reveal You to mankind. He was Emmanuel—'God with us.' God in the flesh. So You *are* a God of mercy, patience, and infinite understanding. Lord, I believe!"

Myles wept for joy.

fifteen

For I determined not to know any thing among you, save Jesus Christ, and him crucified.
1 Corinthians 2:2

His bandaged foot wouldn't fit into a stirrup, so Myles decided to ride Cholla bareback. A wool blanket protected his clothes from her sweat and hair, and he laid his walking stick, a gift from Cyrus Thwaite, across her withers. "Take it easy, Girl," he warned, gripping a hank of her mane in one hand as he sprang to her back and swung his leg over. "I'm running on one foot, so to speak." The swelling had receded and the vivid bruising had faded to pale green and purple, but Myles could put little weight on the foot as yet.

"Myles, you be careful," Virginia called from the front porch as he passed. "Visit your friend and the barber and come straight home. Do you hear?"

"I hear." Reining in the fidgeting mare, Myles grinned at his grandmother. He could endure her motherly domination for the sake of her good cooking and excellent housekeeping skills—abilities he had never before known she possessed. "You're quite a woman, Gram."

"Away with your flattery," she retorted, not before he glimpsed her pleasure.

Cholla trotted almost sideways up the drive, head tucked and tail standing straight up. Its wispy hair streamed behind her like a shredded banner. "You're a loaded weapon today, aren't you?" Myles patted the mare's taut neck. "Sorry; no running. The roads are too icy."

A few miles of trotting took the edge off Cholla's energy. She still occasionally challenged her master's authority, bu her heart was no longer in it. Myles felt her muscles unwind beneath him.

Although it was good to be out in the open again instead of cloistered in his stuffy room, fighting the horse drained much of Myles's strength. When he dismounted in front of Miss Amelia's boardinghouse, he lost hold of his walking stick. It clattered to the frozen mud. Cholla shied to one side, and Myles landed hard. His bad foot hit the ground. Clutching Cholla by the chest and withers, he gritted his teeth and grimaced until the worst pain had passed.

"Steady, Girl," he gasped. Balancing on one foot, he scooped up his stick. It wasn't easy to tether Cholla with one hand, but he managed. Hopping on one foot, using the stick for balance, he made his way to Amelia's porch.

"What on earth are you doing, Myles?" Amelia said, flinging open her front door and ushering him inside.

"I came to see Boz," Myles gasped. "Isn't he here?"

"You come on into the parlor and sit yourself down." Amelia supported his arm with a steely grip. "That's where Boz keeps himself." She lifted her voice. "You got a visitor, Sheriff. Another ailing cowboy on my hands. Just what I needed. You two sit here and have a talk. I've got work to do." Leaving Myles in an armchair, she brushed her hands on her apron, gave each man an affectionate look, and departed.

Boz drew a playing card from his deck, laid it on a stack, and gave Myles a crooked smile. "How's the foot?" His right shoulder was heavily wrapped, binding that arm to his side.

"Mending. You don't sound so good." Myles shifted in his chair.

Boz did not immediately reply. "I ain't so good, Myles," he finally wheezed. "Bullet nicked a lung and severed a nerve in my shoulder. It kinda bounced around in there. Doc did his best, but he doesn't expect I'll regain the use of my arm."

Myles blinked and stared at the floor.

"I know what you're thinkin'," Boz said. "Not much good

in a one-armed sheriff. I reckon God has other plans for my future."

Myles met the other man's steady gaze. Slowly he nodded amazed by Boz's cheerful acceptance of his fate.

"Amelia says I can work for her. She's been needing to hire household help, and she cain't think of anyone she'd rather have about the place."

"You?" Myles stared blankly until he caught the twinkle in his friend's eyes. "Boz, are you joshing me?"

The former sheriff's face creased into a broad grin. "She reckons it wouldn't be proper for me to stay here permanent like, so she proposed marriage."

Myles began to chuckle. Boz put a finger to his lips. "Hush Let the woman think it was all her idea, at least until afte we're hitched."

Myles sputtered with suppressed merriment, and Boz joined in. Soon the two men were wiping tears from thei faces. Boz groaned, holding his shoulder and wheezing. "Sto before you do me in."

The door opened, and Amelia backed into the room carry ing a tray. "I brung you coffee and cakes." Her sharp eye inspected their faces. "Doc says the sheriff needs quiet. Hop I didn't make a mistake by letting you in, Myles."

"He's all right, Amelia. Laughter is good for what ails man. What you got there? Raisin cookies?" Boz perked up.

"Yes, and snickerdoodles. Mind you don't eat more'n i good for ya, Boswell Martin."

Nearly an hour later, Myles grinned as he heaved himsel up on Cholla's back. "Next stop, the store, then on to th barbershop." The horse flicked her ears to listen.

Thank You for leaving Boz with us here on earth, Lord Myles prayed as he rode. *And thank You for giving him hi heart's desire. He's waited a long time for love, but from th look in Amelia's eyes while she fussed over him today, he' found it.*

Myles picked up his mail at the general store. There was

etter addressed in strange handwriting. Curious, he paused ust inside the doorway, balanced on his good foot, and ripped pen the letter.

Dear Myles,

Antonio tells me what to write, and I do my best.

Antonio pray for you every day. He say have you dropped your burden yet? I hope you do, Myles. We want your best for you.

You can write us here in Florida. We stay until summer season open. We want to visit you, but have not the money.

Antonio want to know if the bear was found. He feel bad about keeping it secret. Our circus, it was bought by another man when the owner was put in jail. He cheat one man too many, Antonio say. Things better for us now, but we want a home that does not move.

Antonio speak much of settling down to open a bakery. Is there need for a bakery in your town?

God bless you.

Antonio and Gina Spinelli

Myles determined to write back at his first opportunity. Antonio would be pleased to hear news of his mended relationship with God, and if any town ever needed a bakery, Myles was certain Longtree, Wisconsin, did.

As Myles rode past the parsonage, someone hailed him. He eined in Cholla and waited for the pastor to approach. "Hello, Reverend."

David Schoengard's ruddy face beamed as he stood at Cholla's shoulder and reached up to shake Myles's hand. "Good to see you about town. We've been praying for you. From all I hear, yours was a serious injury."

"Thanks for the prayers. God has been healing me. . .inside and out."

David's eyes gleamed. "Ah, so the lamb has found its way home?"

"More like the Shepherd roped and hog-tied an ornery ram flung it over His shoulder, and hauled it home. I'm afraid I was a tough case, but He never stopped trying to show me the truth."

The pastor chuckled. "I understand. Are you ready to profess your faith before the church?"

Myles tucked his chin. "Is that necessary?"

"Not for your salvation, of course, but it would be a wonderful encouragement to other believers to hear how God worked in your life. I'm also hoping you'll honor us with a song someday soon."

Staring between Cholla's ears, Myles pondered. "I do need to ask forgiveness of people in this town. Guess this is my chance. I'll do it, if you think I should, Reverend."

"I appreciate that—and please call me Dave, or at least Pastor Dave. I'm no more 'reverend' than you are." He patted Cholla's furry neck.

Myles nodded. "All right, Pastor Dave. Do I need your approval on a song?"

"I'll trust you to choose an appropriate selection. And thank you. Caroline will be excited when I tell her you agreed to sing."

"How is she doing?"

"She has a tough time of it during the last weeks before a baby arrives, but she handles it well. My mother is at the house to help out. She and Caroline are great friends."

David cleared his throat. "If you don't mind me asking how are things between you and Marva? Or is it you and Beulah? Caroline and I were never sure."

Myles scratched his beard and took a deep breath. "Marva and I are friends. There never was more between us. And Beulah isn't speaking to me at present. I. . .uh. . .let's just say she got a glimpse of Myles Van Huysen at his worst, and she didn't care much for what she saw."

"I see. Have you apologized?"

"Not yet. I haven't spoken with her since God. . .since He

changed me. I don't know how to approach her. I mean, she pretty much told me to leave her out of my future plans."

"The change in you could make a difference, Myles. Faint heart never won fair maiden."

"Yes, I need to figure out a plan. Right now I'd better be on my way. I've got orders not to dawdle."

"Your grandmother?" David stepped away from the horse. "I enjoyed meeting her last Sunday. Quite a lady."

Myles nodded. "Beulah is a lot like her. Feisty." He smiled. "If you think of it, I could use a few prayers in that area, too. You know, for wisdom and tact when I talk to Beulah."

"Every man needs prayer in the area of communication with women," David said with a straight face. "See you Sunday." With a wink, he turned away.

❦

Myles squirmed in the front pew, elbows resting on his knees, and rubbed one finger across his mustache. His chin felt naked, bereft of its concealing beard. His heart pounded erratically. Lines of a prepared speech raced through his head.

Marva Obermeier played the piano while the congregation sang. She never once looked in his direction. Myles could not sing. He knew he would be ill if he tried. Why had he volunteered to sing so soon? He wasn't ready. It was one thing to entertain a crowd for profit and another thing altogether to sing in worship to God while other believers listened.

"Relax, Myles. The Lord will help you." Virginia leaned over to pat his arm.

He nodded without looking up.

Was Beulah here, somewhere in the room behind him? Would she change her mind when she saw how God was transforming his life, or had he forever frightened her away? With an effort, Myles turned his thoughts and heart back to God and prayed for courage and peace. *This is all new to me, Lord. I feel like a baby, helpless and dependent. Can You really use me?*

His foot throbbed. He needed to prop it up again. Pastor

David was making an announcement. Myles tried to focus his mind.

"A new brother in Christ has something to share with us this morning. Please join me in welcoming Myles Trent Van Huysen into our fellowship of believers."

Myles rose and turned to face the crowd, leaning on his crutch. Expectant, friendly faces met his gaze. He swallowed hard. "Many of you know that I have been living a lie among you these past few years. Today I wish to apologize for my deceit and ask your forgiveness."

There was Beulah, seated between her mother and Eunice. Her dark eyes held encouragement and concern. She pressed three fingers against her trembling lips.

"My grandmother, Virginia Van Huysen, has prayed for me these many long years. She never gave up hope that God would chase me down. I stand before you to confess that I am now a child of God, saved by the shed blood of Jesus Christ. My life, such as it is, belongs to Him forevermore. I do not yet know how or where He will lead, but I know that I will humbly follow." His voice cracked.

Marva sat beside her father in the fourth row. Although her eyes glittered with unshed tears, she gave Myles an encouraging smile.

"I'm having difficulty even talking—don't know how I'll manage to sing. But I want to share my testimony with a song."

He limped to the piano. After leaning his crutch against the wall, he settled on the bench. This piano needed tuning, and several of its keys were missing their ivories. One key sagged below the rest, dead. Myles played a prolonged introduction while begging God to carry him through this ordeal.

Lifting his face, he closed his eyes and began to sing Elizabeth Clephane's beautiful hymn:

"Beneath the cross of Jesus I fain would take my stand. . ."

Myles knew that the Lord's hand was upon him. His voice

rang true and clear. The third verse was his testimony:

"I take, O cross, thy shadow for my abiding place—
I ask no other sunshine than the sunshine of His face;
Content to let the world go by, to know no gain nor loss,
My sinful self my only shame, my glory all the cross."

The last notes faded away. Myles opened his eyes. His grandmother was beaming, wiping her face with a handkerchief. He collected his crutch and stood. Someone near the back of the room clapped, another person joined in, and soon applause filled the church. "Amen!" Myles recognized Al's voice.

Pastor Schoengard wrapped an arm around Myles's shoulder and asked, "Would anyone like to hear more from our brother?"

The clapping and shouts increased in volume. " 'Amazing Grace.' " It was Cyrus Thwaite's creaky voice.

" 'Holy, Holy, Holy,' " someone else requested.

Pastor David lifted his hand, chuckling. "This is still a worship service, friends. Please maintain order and do not overwhelm our new brother." He turned to Myles. "Will you sing again, or do you need rest?" he asked in an undertone. "Don't feel obliged, Myles. There will be other days."

Myles stared at the floor, dazed by this openhearted reception. He smiled at the pastor. "It is an honor." He returned to the bench and began to play, making the ancient spinet sound like a concert grand.

sixteen

But as it is written, Eye hath not seen, nor ear heard,
neither have entered into the heart of man,
the things which God hath prepared for them that love him.
1 Corinthians 2:9

"Whoa, Girl." Myles hauled the horse to a stop and set the buggy's brake. On the other side of a pasture fence, Al and Buck kept watch over a smoldering fire, feeding it with branches and dead leaves. Smoke shifted across the sodden field, hampered by drifting snowflakes.

Myles hoisted a large basket up to the seat beside him, unlatched the lid, and peeked inside. Indignant yellow eyes met his gaze. "Meow," Pushy complained.

"I'll be right back, I promise. I need to talk to Buck for a minute. You should be warm enough in there." Leaving the basket on the floor, he climbed down and vaulted the fence, hopping on his good foot before regaining his balance.

Cold seeped through his layers of clothing. "Not a great day to be outside," he commented to the other men as he approached. "That fire feels good." He held out gloved hands to the blaze.

"Need to get rid of this brush before winter sets in for good," Buck answered, forking another bundle of dead leaves into the fire. Flames crackled, and ashes drifted upward. "This is the best weather for it. Little danger of fire spreading."

"Um, I need to talk with you, Buck. Do you have a minute?"

Al looked from Myles to Buck and back. "Need privacy? I can head for the house and visit the family."

Myles shifted his weight, winced at the pain in his leg, and tried to smile. "Thanks. Would you take the buggy, Al? I've got Pushy and the kittens with me—planned to let Beulah see them. I'm afraid they'll get cold."

Al smirked and shook his head. "You and those cats! All right, I'll deliver the litter to Beulah, but that's all. Should I tell her you're coming?"

Myles nodded. "Soon."

He stood beside Buck and watched Al drive away. The rooftop of Fairfield's Folly was visible through the leafless trees surrounding it. Smoke drifted from its chimneys. Myles could easily imagine Beulah working at the stove or washing dishes.

"How's the leg?"

"Better every day."

"Good. Violet is in town visiting Caroline and the Schoengard baby," Buck said. "Had you heard? Little girl, arrived last night, big and healthy. They named her Jemima after Pastor David's mother."

"That's wonderful! A healthy girl, eh?" Myles fidgeted. "Great news."

"Beulah is watching Daniel. Samuel stayed home from school; said he was sick. I have my doubts." A smile curled Buck's thick mustache and crinkled the corners of his eyes.

"Beulah is home?"

"That's what I said. Washing laundry, last I saw."

"I, uh, need to talk with you. About the future. I mean, about Beulah and me. I need advice."

Buck threw a branch on the fire. "I'm listening."

Myles shifted his gaze from the fire to the house to the trees and back to Buck. He crossed and uncrossed his arms. "I'm not sure where to begin."

Buck smiled. Sparks flew when he tossed a large pine knot into the blaze.

"I want to ask your permission to marry Beulah, but I don't know how soon I'll be able to support a wife. I must return to New York and give a concert tour. Along with a few remaining stocks and bonds and whatever is left from the sale of the family house after I pay off debts, the money I earn should be enough to purchase the Thwaite farm. Cyrus agreed to hold it for me. . .at least for a few months." Myles spoke rapidly. Realizing that he was rubbing the front of his coat, he stuffed the errant hand into his pocket.

"Do you plan to propose before you leave or after you return?"

"I don't know." Myles rubbed the back of his neck, pushing his hat over his forehead. "Do you think she will accept my proposal at all? I mean, I haven't spoken with her—not a real conversation—since the time she blew up at me. I can't leave without knowing, but at the same time it would be tough to leave her behind once we're engaged. What do you think I ought to do, Buck?"

"Have you prayed about this?"

"God must be sick of my voice by now. I've been begging for wisdom and guidance. I feel so puny and stupid. After years of regarding God with—I'm embarrassed to admit this, but it's the truth—with a superior attitude, I'm feeling like small potatoes these days."

"God likes small potatoes. They are useful to Him."

Myles shoved his hat back into place. His smile felt unsteady, as did his knees. "If Beulah won't have me, I'll set up housekeeping with my grandmother. Gram has decided she likes Longtree better than New York, believe it or not. Most of her old friends have died, and she prefers to live out her earthly days with me here. She's a great lady."

"That she is. And what are her plans if you marry?"

"She would be willing either to settle in town at Miss Amelia's boardinghouse or to stay with us at the farm, whichever Beulah would prefer. Gram has money of her own, enough to keep her in modest comfort for life." Myles tossed a handful of twigs into the fire, one at a time. "Do you. . .do you think Beulah will see me today? I mean, is she still angry? I was terrible to her that day—I swore at her, threatened her, and manhandled her."

Buck shook his head. A little chuckle escaped.

"What are you thinking?" Myles asked in frustration.

"Beulah and her mother have been sewing a wedding gown these past few weeks while you've been stewing in remorse and uncertainty. She forgave you even before you professed your faith at church. Beulah's temper is quick, but she seldom holds a grudge. I hope you know what a moody little firebrand you're getting. That girl will require plenty of loving attention."

Myles gaped as a glow spread throughout his soul. "She's been making a wedding dress? For me?"

"Actually, I believe she intends to wear it herself," Buck said dryly.

Myles was too intent to be amused. "And I have your permission to propose?"

"You do. Violet and I are well acquainted with your industry and fidelity, my friend. You will be an excellent husband to our girl."

Myles stared at the ground, blinking hard. "And I had the gall to believe God had deserted me," he mumbled. Biting his lip, he turned away. "I don't deserve this."

Buck wrapped a strong arm around the younger man's shoulders. "I felt the same way when Violet accepted me."

"You did?"

Buck laughed aloud. "Go talk to the girl and decide together on a wedding date. It might be wiser to wait until your return from New York to marry; but then again it might be pleasant for the two of you to make that concert tour together—a kind of paid honeymoon. Beulah could be your inspiration."

Myles stared into space until Buck gave him a shove. "Get on with you. She's waiting."

❦

Beulah jabbed a clothespin into place, securing Samuel's overalls on the cord Papa had suspended across the kitchen. The laundry nearest the stove steamed. Beulah tested one of Daniel's diapers. It was still damp.

"You could at least try to talk to me," she accused the absent Myles. "How am I supposed to demonstrate unselfish love to a man I never see?" Her lips trembled. Clenching her jaw, she stabbed another clothespin at an undervest but missed. "No one tells me anything. For all I know, he's going back to New York without me."

Recalling Myles's singing in church, she brushed a tear away with the back of one hand. "He was so handsome. I hardly knew him without his beard. He looked like a stranger. And oh his song made my soul ache." Pressing a hand to her breast, she allowed a quiet sob. "You have changed his heart, haven't You God? Mama was so right. After all my accusations that Mama wouldn't give Myles a chance, *I'm* the one who quit on him at the crucial moment. Please let me try again, Lord."

Samuel's wool sock joined its mate on the line.

A whimper of sound escaped as Beulah's lips moved. "If you have changed your mind about me, the least you could do is come and tell me so. Oh, Myles, I love you so much!"

A lid rattled. "Who are you talking to, Beulah?" Samuel slipped an oatmeal cookie from the crock and took an enormous bite. Watchful sat at his feet, tail waving, hopeful eyes fixed upon the cookie.

Startled to discover that she was not alone, Beulah glared. "Myself."

"Finally found someone who wants to listen, hmm?" Samuel ducked when she threw a wet towel at his head. Laughing, he left the kitchen with Watchful at his heels.

"I thought you were too sick to go to school," Beulah yelled after him. "You'd better get in bed before Mama comes home."

She retrieved the towel, brushing off dust. Sighing, she decided it needed washing again. "My penalty for a temper tantrum."

Scraping damp hair from her face with water-shriveled fingers, she drifted to the window and stared outside. Movement drew her attention to her garden. A doe and two large fawns, dressed in their gray winter coats, nibbled at bolted cabbages. Resting her arms on the windowsill, Beulah felt her heart lighten. "Better not let anyone else see you," she warned the deer. "One of your former companions is hanging on the meat hook by the barn. We have plenty of venison for the winter, but you never know."

The animals' ears twitched. All three stared toward Beulah's window. After a tense moment, the doe flicked her tail and returned to her browsing. Then the three deer lifted their heads to stare toward the barn before springing away into the forest.

Watchful barked from the entryway, and Beulah heard a man's deep voice. Her hands flew to her messy hair, and her eyes widened.

"Al is here!" Samuel shouted. "He brought something in a basket."

"I'll be right there," she said, relaxing. It was only Al. "Why aren't you in bed, Sam?"

Samuel pounded upstairs, skipping steps on the way.

❦

Myles lifted his hand to knock just as the door opened. Al waved an arm to usher him inside. "Enter, please. I'm on my way out. I'll take my mare back and leave the buggy for you. Want me to stable Bess before I go?"

Myles nodded as he limped inside. "Thanks, Al." He swallowed hard. "Where is Beulah?"

Al's grin widened. "In the parlor. Sitting on your bear."

"My bear?" Myles stopped, puzzled.

"It makes a nice rug."

"Oh, the bear."

Shaking his head, Al laughed. "Go on. Talking to you is useless." He clapped his hat on his head and slammed the door as he left.

Myles licked his lips and took a fortifying breath. *Lord, please help me.*

He stepped into the parlor. A shaggy brown rug lay before the stone hearth. Beulah sat Indian style in the middle of the bear's back, and in the hammock of her skirt lay Pushy and four tiny kittens. Firelight glowed in Beulah's eyes and hair. The cat purred with her eyes closed while her babies nursed.

"Myles!" Beulah's voice held all the encouragement Myles required. "You came."

Daniel lay on his back near the rug, waving a wooden rattle with one hand. At the sight of Myles, the baby rolled to his stomach and called a cheerful greeting. Myles bent to pick up the baby, enjoying the feel of his solid little body. Daniel crowed again and whacked Myles in the face with a slimy hand. Bouncing for joy, he dropped his rattle.

"I came. You like my kittens?" Favoring his left leg, he settled near her on the rug. Daniel wriggled out of his grasp and scooted toward the fallen toy. "I wanted you to see them before their eyes opened."

"They are adorable." Beulah lifted a black and white kitten. Its pink feet splayed, and its mouth opened in a silent meow. Pushy opened her eyes partway until Beulah returned her baby. "I love them, Myles."

Hearing a catch in her voice, he inspected her face. "What's wrong?"

"Does this mean you're leaving? You brought the kittens to me for safekeeping."

Myles noted the dots of perspiration on her pert nose, the quivering of her full lips. Tenderness seemed to swell his heart until he could scarcely draw breath. "No, my dearest. I simply wanted you to see them. I have just spoken to your stepfather, as your mother wisely advised."

Beulah's dark eyes held puzzlement. "You spoke to Papa?"

"Have you changed your mind, Beulah? Do you still wish to marry me? Can you forgive me for swearing at you and threatening you?"

She clasped her hands at her breast. "Yes, Myles! More than anything I want to marry you!" She started to rise then remembered the burden in her lap.

Chuckling, Myles scrambled to his hands and knees, leaned over, and kissed her gently. Below his chest, Pushy's purring increased in volume.

When he pulled away, Beulah's eyelashes fluttered. Her

lips were still parted. He returned to place a kiss on her nose. "We need to talk, Honey."

"Your mustache tickles."

Just then, Daniel let out a squawk. Startled, Myles and Beulah turned. Only the baby's feet projected from beneath the davenport.

"Oh, Daniel!" Beulah cried. "He rolled under there again. Would you get him, Myles?" She deposited kitten after kitten in the blanket-lined basket. Pushy hopped in and curled up with her brood.

After crawling across the room, Myles took hold of Daniel's feet and pulled him out from under the davenport. As soon as he saw Myles, Daniel grinned. "You're a pretty decent chaperone, Fella," Myles said. "Better than Pushy is, at any rate."

Beulah hurried to scoop up her dusty brother. "He moves so quickly. I got used to him staying in one place, but now he's into everything."

"Can I come in yet? Are you done kissing?" Poised in the parlor doorway, Samuel wore a pained expression.

"Don't count on it," Myles said.

Beulah shrugged. "You might as well join us. You're no more sick than I am, you scamp. But at least this way you get to be first to hear our news: Myles and I are getting married."

Samuel stretched out on the bearskin, combing its fur with his fingers. "I know. I heard you."

"You were listening? Samuel, how could you?"

"Easy enough. I was sitting on the stairs." He lifted a gray kitten from the basket and cradled it against his face.

While Beulah gasped with indignation, Myles began to chuckle. He sat on the davenport and patted the seat beside him. "Come on, Honey. It doesn't matter. We've got important things to discuss." After depositing Daniel on the rug for Samuel to entertain, Beulah snuggled beneath Myles's arm and soon regained her good humor.

While Samuel played with kittens and Daniel rolled about on the floor, the lovers planned their future.

epilogue

January 1882, New York City

Curled into the depths of a well-cushioned sofa, Beulah shut her book, smiling. Snow drifted upon the balcony outside her window, mounding on the railings like fine white sugar. Closing her eyes, she sighed in contentment. *Thank You, Lord. Married life is better than I ever imagined.*

The Van Huysens had opted to stay in one of the older hotels in the city. Its old-fashioned splendor was sufficient to please Beulah without overwhelming her. At times, especially around the holidays, she had suffered pangs of homesickness. But Myles's adoration, combined with the knowledge that this tour was temporary, soothed her occasional feelings of inadequacy and loneliness.

She slipped a letter from inside the book cover. There on the envelope her new name, "Mrs. Myles Van Huysen," was written in Mama's neat script. Beulah ran her finger over the words. She was eager to share family news with Myles that night after the concert. He was currently at the theater, practicing.

"Beulah?" A familiar voice called from outside the hotel door. Virginia did not believe in knocking. Beulah hurried to let in her new grandmother.

Virginia bustled into the room, her arms filled with packages. "I've been shopping. Wish you had come with me, but I still managed to spend a good deal. I want you to try this on." After dropping several boxes upon a table, she shoved the largest in Beulah's direction.

"What have you done, Gram?" Beulah chuckled. "What will Myles say?"

"I don't care what that boy might say. It's my money, and

I'll spend it as I like." Spying the letter in Beulah's hand, she said, "So you've heard from your mother again? How is everyone back home?"

The crisp inquiry warmed Beulah's heart. She kissed Virginia's cheek. "I love you, Gram. Mama says to tell you 'hello.' They are all well. Daniel is pulling up to stand beside furniture now. Sheriff Boz and Miss Amelia have set February fourteenth as their wedding day, so we should be home in time for the wedding. Um, let's see. . .Eunice found homes for all four of Pushy's kittens. Mama and Papa are letting her keep the black one, Miss Amelia chose the black and white girl, and Mr. Thwaite picked the gray boy. Believe it or not, Al decided to take the black one with white feet! After all his teasing Myles about liking cats, he now has a pet cat of his own."

"That's so nice, Dear." Virginia smiled fondly at the girl. "Only a few days now until we'll all be on the train headed for Wisconsin."

"Will you be sorry to leave New York? You must miss your old house. Didn't it hurt to see strangers take it over?"

Virginia pursed her lips and gazed through the window at blowing snow. "For many years now New York has not seemed like home. Ever since the boys left me, I've been a lonely soul. My friends are all gone, and sometimes when I walked around that old house, I missed my dear husband Edwin so much. . . . I could picture John and Gwendolyn chasing up and down the stairs—they were our only children, you know. John was killed in the war, and Gwen died of cholera at age fifteen."

Shaking her head, she said firmly, "Dwelling in the past is detrimental to one's mental and spiritual health. Now I have Myles, you, and many friends in Longtree." Her expression brightened. "My life is in the future now. First in Wisconsin, then in heaven!"

Seeing Beulah dab at a tear, she started back into action. "Now take these boxes and try on the gown. It's only a short time 'til we must leave for the theater. Don't want to be late! I

had a note from Mr. Poole this morning—he will be at th
concert tonight. The man seems to take personal pleasure i
Myles's success, which is not too strange considering his rol
in the boy's return to the stage. I hear it's another sold-ou
house. Myles's agent has been begging him to reconsider an
stay on permanently."

Arms loaded with boxes, Beulah turned back to grin. "Poo
man! He hasn't a chance against Cyrus Thwaite's farm."

❦

Beulah perched on the edge of her seat, absently fanning her
self. Her emerald taffeta evening gown rustled with ever
movement, but it was impossible to keep entirely still.

"Hard to believe it's snowing outside, isn't it?" Virgini
leaned over to ask. She smoothed a bit of lace on Beulah'
shoulder and smiled approval.

Beulah nodded in reply. The old lady's whispers wer
sometimes louder than she intended. Myles was singing
heart-wrenching aria from *Aida*, and Beulah wanted to listen.

"Hard to believe this is the last week of Myles's tour,
Virginia commented a few minutes later while Myles per
formed Schumann's A Minor Piano Concerto. Again, Beula
nodded briefly.

After weeks of attending her husband's concerts, she sti
had not tired of hearing him sing and play. Each night Myle
varied his repertoire. Always he sang opera, usually Verdi o
Mozart; often he performed a few ballads and popular songs
most nights he took requests from the audience. Beulah'
favorite part of each performance was discovering whic
hymn he would choose for his finale.

Tonight he sang "Holy, Holy, Holy." Beulah closed her eye
to listen without distraction. No matter how cross, irritating
or obstinate Myles might have been during the day, each nigh
she fell in love with him all over again. He was so handsome
charming, and irresistible up on that stage!

"I think I'll head home now, Dear," Virginia said whil
Myles took his bow.

Beulah stopped clapping long enough to return the old ady's kiss. "Thank you so much for this marvelous dress, and he gloves, and the reticule, and everything! Your taste is xquisite. You are too good to me." Beulah smoothed the ruf-les on her bouffant skirt.

"Child, it was my pleasure. I trust Myles will approve. I ope you know how thankful I am to have you for a grand-laughter. Myles has excellent taste, too. Good night." She atted Beulah's cheek and bustled away. Although Myles ften requested her to let him escort her home, Virginia main-ained independence, insisting that she was perfectly capable f hailing a cab and returning alone to the hotel.

As soon as the red velvet curtain fell, Beulah gathered her hings and hurried backstage. Myles waited for her in his ressing room, smiling in welcome.

"Do you like it?" Beulah twirled in place. "Gram bought it or me. Isn't she wonderful? Not that I'll find much use for an vening gown back in Longtree. Gram fixed my hair, too."

Myles's eyes glowed. "You are beautiful, my Beulah. More han any man deserves." His voice was slightly hoarse.

When he closed the door behind her, Beulah wrapped her rms around her husband's neck and kissed him. "Thank you, hank you for bringing me with you to New York. I wouldn't ave missed this experience for the world," she murmured gainst his lips.

"You say that every night," he chuckled, pressing her slen-ler form close.

"And every night I mean it," she insisted. Framing his face vith her hands, she studied each feature. "Sometimes I miss our beard, but I do love how your face feels right after you have."

"You're standing on my feet." He rubbed his smooth cheek gainst hers.

"That way I'm taller." She stood on tiptoe to kiss him.

He took her by the waist and lifted her off his feet. "How bout if I bend over instead? These shoes were expensive, and my toes are irreplaceable." Smiling, he kissed her pouting lips

Consoled, Beulah snuggled against him. "Darling, some times I don't want this honeymoon to end; other times I wan so much to be back in Longtree, setting up our new home But it will be hard to return to ordinary life after all this glitte and glamour."

"This has been a marvelous honeymoon tour, but I think w would soon tire of such a hectic lifestyle. Think of snowba fights, ice-skating on the beaver pond, and toasting chestnuts We need to hike up the stream and visit our waterfall whil it's frozen."

"And I am looking forward to experiencing everyday thing as your wife," Beulah added. "Cooking breakfast for you i our own kitchen, washing your laundry, collecting eggs fron our own chickens."

Myles hugged her close and rocked her back and forth Secure in his arms, Beulah felt entirely loved.

"Yes, each day offers its own pleasures," he mused alouc "Be content with the joys of today, Darling. This tour has bee successful beyond my wildest dreams. I know God paved th way, and I'm sure we can trust Him to plan the rest of ou future as well. We're making memories right now that we'l treasure for the rest of our lives. God is very good."

A Letter To Our Readers

Dear Reader:

In order that we might better contribute to your reading enjoyment, we would appreciate your taking a few minutes to respond to the following questions. We welcome your comments and read each form and letter we receive. When completed, please return to the following:

Rebecca Germany, Fiction Editor
Heartsong Presents
PO Box 719
Uhrichsville, Ohio 44683

1. Did you enjoy reading *Myles from Anywhere* by Jill Stengl?
   - ❑ Very much! I would like to see more books by this author!
   - ❑ Moderately. I would have enjoyed it more if

   ____

   ____

   ____

2. Are you a member of **Heartsong Presents**? Yes ❑ No ❑
   If no, where did you purchase this book? ______________

   ____

3. How would you rate, on a scale from 1 (poor) to 5 (superior), the cover design? ______________________

4. On a scale from 1 (poor) to 10 (superior), please rate the following elements.

_____ Heroine	_____ Plot
_____ Hero	_____ Inspirational theme
_____ Setting	_____ Secondary characters

5. These characters were special because ______________________

____

____

6. How has this book inspired your life? ______________________

____

____

7. What settings would you like to see covered in future **Heartsong Presents** books? ______________________

____

____

8. What are some inspirational themes you would like to see treated in future books? ______________________

____

____

9. Would you be interested in reading other **Heartsong Presents** titles? Yes ❑ No ❑

10. Please check your age range:

❑ Under 18 ❑ 18-24 ❑ 25-34

❑ 35-45 ❑ 46-55 ❑ Over 55

Name ______________________________________

Occupation ________________________________

Address ___________________________________

City ____________________ State ______________ Zip ____________

Email _____________________________________

Yellow Roses

Texas Rangers are the pride of the Lone Star state as law officers, not as sons-in-law. Few parents welcome a courting ranger, with his hard, dangerous life. Who would want his daughter involved with a lawman of the Old West, in a state full of characters willing to break the law in any possible way?

Relive the Old West with the men who protected it and the courageous women who stood by them. With their lives ultimately in God's hands, these women will rise to the call of love.

paperback, 352 pages, 5 3/16" x 8"

♥ ♥ ♥ ♥ ♥ ♥ ♥ ♥ ♥ ♥ ♥ ♥ ♥ ♥ ♥ ♥ ♥

Please send me ____ copies of *Yellow Roses*. I am enclosing $5.97 for each.
Please add $2.00 to cover postage and handling per order. OH add 6% tax.

Send check or money order, no cash or C.O.D.s please.

Name____

Address______________________________________

City, State, Zip________________________________

To place a credit card order, call 1-800-847-8270.

Send to: Heartsong Presents Reader Service, PO Box 721, Uhrichsville, OH 44683

♥ ♥ ♥ ♥ ♥ ♥ ♥ ♥ ♥ ♥ ♥ ♥ ♥ ♥ ♥ ♥ ♥